Peter closed his eyes and pictured himself carrying Ellen to his bed....

Suddenly the word *virgin* flashed into his mind. For a moment, the male animal in him reveled at the thought of being the first man to possess her. Then a chill of reality swept over him. Did he want that responsibility? Ellen had waited a long time for Mr. Right. Peter couldn't take her in a moment of weakness....

He stepped back, releasing her completely.

"I told you that you were safe here. And I'm a man of my word. You came here a virgin. You'll leave here as one." Before she had time to respond, he headed back to the loft. *That was the hardest thing I've ever done,* he admitted. And he knew he would never have the strength to do it again....

Dear Reader,

This month, Romance is chock-full of excitement. First, VIRGIN BRIDES continues with *The Bride's Second Thought*, an emotionally compelling story by bestselling author Elizabeth August. When a virginal bride-to-be finds her fiancé with another woman, she flees to the mountains for refuge...only to be stranded with a gorgeous stranger who gives her second thoughts about a lot of things....

Next, Natalie Patrick offers up a delightful BUNDLES OF JOY with *Boot Scootin' Secret Baby*. Bull rider Jacob "Cub" Goodacre returns to South Dakota for his rodeo hurrah, only to learn he's still a married man...and father to a two-year-old heart tugger. BACHELOR GULCH, Sandra Steffen's wonderful Western series, resumes with the story of an estranged couple who had wed for the sake of their child...but wonder if they can rekindle their love in *Nick's Long-Awaited Honeymoon*.

Rising star Kristin Morgan delivers a tender, sexy tale about a woman whose biological clock is booming and the best friend who consents to being her *Shotgun Groom*. If you want a humorous—red-hot!—read, try Vivian Leiber's *The 6'2", 200 lb. Challenge*. The battle of the sexes doesn't get any better! Finally, Lisa Kaye Laurel's fairy-tale series, ROYAL WEDDINGS, draws to a close with *The Irresistible Prince,* where the woman hired to find the royal a wife realizes *she* is the perfect candidate!

In May, VIRGIN BRIDES resumes with Annette Broadrick, and future months feature titles by Suzanne Carey and Judy Christenberry, among others. So keep coming back to Romance, where you're sure to find the classic tales you love, told in fresh, exciting ways.

Enjoy!

Joan Marlow Golan

Joan Marlow Golan
Senior Editor, Silhouette Romance

Please address questions and book requests to:
Silhouette Reader Service
U.S.: 3010 Walden Ave., P.O. Box 1325, Buffalo, NY 14269
Canadian: P.O. Box 609, Fort Erie, Ont. L2A 5X3

VIRGIN BRIDES

THE BRIDE'S SECOND THOUGHT

Elizabeth August

Silhouette
ROMANCE™
Published by Silhouette Books
America's Publisher of Contemporary Romance

SILHOUETTE BOOKS

ISBN 0-373-19288-6

THE BRIDE'S SECOND THOUGHT

Printed in U.S.A.

Books by Elizabeth August

Silhouette Romance

ELIZABETH AUGUST

lives in western North Carolina with her husband, Doug, and her three boys, Douglas, Benjamin and Matthew. She began writing romances soon after Matthew was born. She's always wanted to write.

Elizabeth does counted cross-stitching to keep from eating at night. It doesn't always work. "I love to bowl, but I'm not very good. I keep my team's handicap high. I like hiking in the Shenadoahs, as long as we start up the mountain so the return trip is down rather than vice versa." She loves to go to Cape Hatteras to watch the sun rise over the ocean. Elizabeth August has also published under the pseudonym Betsy Page.

Dear Reader,

I have been called old-fashioned and naive. I'll accept old-fashioned because in many ways I am…at least as defined by the modern media. I confess, I saved myself for marriage, and my family has always come first.

As for being naive, I am not. Considering the threats to one's health and the possibility of an unexpected pregnancy, I considered my choice to remain chaste a rational one. Certainly a safe one. And, because I am the person I am, it was the right emotional choice for me. Other women have made a different choice, and it has worked out just as well for them. And I am happy for them.

To those of you reading this letter, my hope is that you will listen to *your* heart and mind and do what's best for *you*. And I sincerely wish each and every one of you a long and happy life.

Best,

Elizabeth August

Chapter One

"Stupid! Stupid! Stupid! Stupid!" Ellen Reese muttered to herself. "Decisions made at 2:00 a.m. should always be reevaluated in the light of day."

Of course she'd had all day to think, but she'd been too angry and hurt. The truth was she hadn't wanted to think. Now she was in trouble and had no one to blame but herself.

When she'd left Boston this morning, the sky had been clear. Halfway through New Hampshire, fresh snow had begun to fall but she hadn't stopped. For a foolish reason that had seemed rational at two in the morning, she'd vowed to keep driving until she'd crossed the Canadian border. So she'd continued north through the mountainous terrain, concentrating on the beauty of the white-blanketed wilderness and trying to block out the scene that had sent her on this journey.

She'd reasoned that she didn't have to worry about a few flakes. There was already several feet of snow on the ground. People up here were used to snow. The highway department had plenty of plows to clear the roadways. After all, this was ski country and people made their money catering to tourists. Besides, if the roads got dangerous, she could always find a motel.

With those thoughts in mind, she hadn't paid any heed to the increasing strength of the storm nor the steadily increasing buildup of snow on the road. Admittedly, when she'd passed through that last small town, she had considered stopping, but the border was so close, and getting there had become an obsession. Minutes ago the snow had suddenly begun to come down with blizzard force. Blocking out the remaining rays of daylight, it had brought with it an early dusk. Even with her windshield wipers moving rapidly, she'd barely been able to see beyond the hood of her car and had had to reduce her speed to a crawl. She'd considered turning back but, according to the map, there was another town not much further in front of her. Besides, since she was hardly able to see forward, making a U-turn with no visibility hadn't appealed to her.

It was about that time that the extent of the foolishness of her behavior had hit her full force. Straining her eyes, looking for evidence of other cars on the road, she'd recalled that she'd seem none for quite a while. Even in the small town she'd passed through, no one had been out.

"That's because everyone else was smart enough to stay in or seek shelter a long time ago," she'd admonished herself.

Driving had become more and more impossible. Out of desperation, when she'd seen a mailbox, she'd turned off the main road onto the private lane hoping to seek shelter at the home beyond.

Now she was hopelessly stuck. Even worse, she couldn't see any indication of a house in the distance. The lane simply wound into the forest.

Fighting a rising panic, she peered hard into the dim twilight. The lane had been plowed after the last snowfall. She could tell that because of the mounds of snow on either side. That meant that someone lived out there somewhere.

"The house is probably just around the first bend," she reasoned, using the sound of her voice to bolster her courage.

Wrapping her coat tightly around her body, she opened the car door and stepped out. A blast of arctic air greeted her. Feeling her feet already beginning to freeze, she silently congratulated herself for not being entirely foolish and popped open the trunk. She'd been driving in sneakers but had packed boots. Finding them and grabbing her suitcase, she climbed into the back seat. There in the shelter of her vehicle, she discarded her sneakers and wet socks. A strong gust of wind buffeted the car causing it to sway. After finding a pair of fresh socks, she pulled them on, then pulled on the boots. Already snow had covered her front windshield.

"Maybe it would be smart to wait until daylight or at least until the snow stops," she murmured under her breath. Her short trip to the trunk had left her coat snow covered and a chill creeping through her body. If she remained where she was, she had a suitcase full of clothes she could keep layering to stay warm.

"Or I could end up freezing to death in the back seat of my car when there could be a house no more than a hundred yards away," she argued, feeling the temperature of the interior of the vehicle dropping rapidly.

Suddenly the car jolted. Looking to the window beside her, she saw a pair of huge paws spread on the glass.

A gasp of fear escaped. Then recognizing the paws as belonging to a canine, she reminded herself that dogs had masters, and her fear was replaced by a flood of relief.

A long wolflike snout and sharp bared teeth became visible between the paws.

"I think I'll just wait in the car until his master arrives," she decided, hoping the glass would hold.

The animal lowered itself and took a stance a couple of feet away. Peering out the window, her breath caught in her throat. She'd assumed the dog was the pet of the people who owned the house the mailbox belonged to. But on closer inspection, it looked more like a wolf. "Some breeds of dogs look like wolves," she reasoned encouragingly. Still, recalling that wolves ran in packs, she peered out all of the other windows to see if there were any others. She could see none, but then her visibility was extremely limited.

"It's a dog," she proclaimed, fighting to keep her panic from rising.

Suddenly the animal lifted its chin and began to howl. *It was a wolf, and it was calling to its friends!* For a moment she sat frozen in fear, then her fighting instinct took over. "Think!" she ordered herself.

"I've got to believe there's someone just around that bend," she said through clenched teeth. Leaning over the front seat, she paused with her hand above the horn. Was an SOS three dots, three dashes and three dots or was it three dashes, three dots and three dashes? The first, she decided, and pressed on the horn. After the forth repetition, she stopped. She didn't want to wear out her battery. She'd wait. If no one came, she'd try again when the snow stopped.

The cold was creeping into her bones. Forcing herself to discard her coat momentarily, she pulled on a bulky sweater over the one she was already wearing and a pair of sweatpants over her jeans, then put her coat back on.

Outside the wolf continued to howl.

"Well, if he thinks he's found dinner for his pack, he'd better think again." Her jaw firmed as she checked the locks on the doors, then snuggled more tightly against the back seat.

Above the wind and the beast, another sound caught her attention. It was a motor. Quickly leaning over her front seat, she switched on her lights. Coming down the lane was a snowmobile. The driver threw his arm up in front of his face and, realizing she'd nearly blinded him with her lights, she switched them off. Suddenly afraid for her rescuer, she looked for the wolf. He was running toward the approaching machine.

Moving rapidly, she unlocked her door and stepped out of the car. "Watch out!" she screamed at the top of her lungs, then looked around for a weapon to help the driver fend off the beast and any of his companions that might be arriving soon.

The driver made no move to take any precautions, and she feared her warning had been covered by the sound of the motor. Panic threatened rational thought. Refusing to allow another person to be harmed because of her, she started forward intending to lend assistance to subdue the animal. But as the driver came to a halt and turned off the machine, the beast nuzzled the man's leg, and he reached down and ruffled the wolf's fur.

She'd let her imagination cause her to panic! It was a dog after all. It simply resembled a wolf.

Approaching her, the driver looked at her car and then at her. He was wearing a heavy parka. What she could see of his face was obscured by a full beard and mustache while his bulk was large enough to provide a buffer to the driving snow. The phrase "a mountain of a man" came to mind.

Peter studied the woman. The strain on her face gave the impression of a lost stray tossed out into the cold to fend for itself. Where women were concerned, looks could be deceiving, he reminded himself. "Only an idiot would be out on a night like this," he finally said.

Ellen wanted to feel indignant, but her sanity had returned. "You're right," she admitted, and was certain she sensed surprise on his part.

His gaze shifted to the car. "You're not going to be going anywhere in that for a while." Then he turned back to her. "You'll have to come with me."

As he started toward the snowmobile, she remained in place. Until today, she'd lived by certain rules. And not going home with men she didn't know was a very big one.

Reaching the snowmobile, he turned back. Seeing her where he'd left her, his frown deepened. "You have two choices. You can stay here and turn into an ice sculpture, or you can come home with me."

The snow was matting the length of her body. That, plus a frigid blast of wind that nearly knocked her over, made her decision for her. Where there was life, there was hope, she told herself. And staying here, she was certain to die from exposure. "I need my purse and suitcase," she called back, already on her way to retrieve them.

Trudging after her, he took the suitcase from her. "There's no way you can hold on to that and me at the same time. I'll come back for it," he said, tossing it inside the car.

His manner left no room for compromise. Following him to the snowmobile, she was aware of his pet watching her. The animal's scrutiny added to her nervousness. "I don't think your dog likes me."

"He's a wolf, and he's not mine. He belongs to a friend of mine. So does the cabin we're going to." Peter motioned for the wolf to come closer. "Friend," he said firmly. "Now home!"

The wolf took off at a run down the lane.

After brushing the snow from the seat, Peter climbed onto the snowmobile. Ellen climbed on behind him. With nothing else to hold on to, she was forced to wrap her arms around his waist. As they started down the lane, she'd intended to stay as far from her rescuer as possible. But the bitter wind changed her mind. Huddling against his back, she let his bulk protect her.

The lane wound through the forest for what seemed like forever. Just when she was beginning to wonder if there was a cabin, she smelled wood smoke. Peering around the broad shoulder protecting her from the elements, she saw a clearing with a building in the center. As they drew closer she realized it was a real log cabin.

The wolf shook the snow off its coat as Ellen and the stranger mounted the porch steps. Her rescuer also paused on the porch to brush himself off and stomp some of the snow off his boots. She followed his example before entering behind the wolf.

The interior of the cabin was a pleasant surprise. Considering her companion's mountain man appearance, she'd expected something totally rustic. Instead, the furniture was comfortable looking, and there was a cozy atmosphere. A fireplace with logs blazing was to one side. A couch and chair grouping fronted it. Toward the back was a kitchen section with a heavy wooden table and chairs. Above the fireplace area was a loft. Three doors led off the central living area. One was ajar, and she saw a bed.

"The bathroom's over there." Peter motioned toward one of the two closed doors. "I'll be back with your suitcases in a little while. Is there anything else you want from your car?"

Feeling guilty about sending him out into the storm, she said hurriedly, "There's really no need for you to go out there again. I can get along fine until tomorrow, and then I'll be on my way."

At least she wasn't spoiled, Peter thought. The last thing he wanted was to be cloistered with a demanding female. "There's no way to be certain when we'll get dug out up here. The snow is supposed to continue through the night, and, with the way the wind is blowing, it'll probably drift up onto your car. If I wait, I'll have to dig out your car just to get to your luggage. Now, is there anything else you want?"

She realized that arguing would be futile. "There's an overnight bag in the trunk."

He extended his hand for her keys. As soon as she dropped them into his palm, he left.

Turning to look out the window, she saw him remount the snowmobile and disappear into the snowy night. She'd hoped there would be a wife and children in the cabin, but there didn't appear to be anyone else here. Recalling that he'd said the place belonged to a friend, she called out a hello. There was no answer. Apparently, it was going to be just her, the man and the wolf. This thought caused an uneasy curl to work its way through her. "You've gotten yourself into a fine mess," she grumbled at herself.

Suddenly afraid that the wolf would decide she wasn't a friend after all, her gaze swung to the fireplace. The animal was lying near the hearth, his head up, watching her, as if wondering if he should trust her or not.

"Don't worry, I don't intend to take anything or stay long," she assured him.

He lowered his head onto his paws, but his gaze remained on her.

Moving slowly, not wanting to give him any reason for alarm, she removed her coat and hung it on one of the pegs by the door. Next came the boots. As she took off the sweatpants, she congratulated herself for having put them on. The snow had clung to them and, still unmelted, its dampness had not yet penetrated to her jeans.

Nature called and she headed to the bathroom. It was larger than she'd expected and clean. There was an old-fashioned, legged bathtub and all the other amenities. The faint scent of aftershave reminded her of her rescuer.

She hadn't gotten a very good look at him when they'd entered the cabin. In fact all she'd really noticed was a pair of the deepest blue eyes she'd ever seen... impatient, reproving blue eyes.

Leaving the bathroom, she walked slowly around the main living area, taking stock of her surroundings. A quick peek in the second room with a closed door revealed a study. Two walls were lined with filled bookshelves. There was a desk with an elaborate computer in front of the window. On the other side wall was another desk with a ham radio. Climbing the ladder to the loft she found a mattress up there and guessed this was the guest quarters.

"Nice place," she addressed the wolf as she descended to the main floor. She'd been aware that the animal's gaze had never left her.

He made no response.

Her body finally warming, the second sweater she was wearing was beginning to feel unnecessary. Stripping it off, she settled onto the couch. But she didn't relax. Guilt for having allowed her rescuer to again go out in the storm plagued her. She told herself that he was obviously used to this kind of weather. Still, her anxiousness increased. The wind was blowing even more forcefully now, producing an angry wrathlike howl. Crossing to the window, she peered out at the night. The snow was falling so thickly, she could barely see beyond the rail of the roofed porch.

"He'll be all right," she said aloud, using the sound of her voice to bolster her courage. Glancing toward the wolf, she saw him continuing to watch her. "Well, I told him he didn't have to go out," she said in her defense.

Suddenly the wolf was on its feet, and the fear that it had decided she wasn't a friend caused her legs to weaken. Then, above the storm, she heard the sound of a motor. A moment later she saw a faint light and breathed a sigh of relief.

She opened the door when the man reached the porch. "Thanks," she said as he entered and set her suitcase and overnight bag on the floor, then removed his coat.

Sitting down in a nearby chair, Peter concentrated on taking off his boots. "You're welcome."

The relief she'd been feeling proved fleeting. Beneath his heavy coat, her rescuer was wearing a heavy red plaid flannel shirt over a white turtleneck. Despite the layering, she could see his shoulders were broad, and as he bent to unlace his boots, there was no evidence of a potbelly getting in his way. His jeans fit snugly around muscular thighs, and she guessed that with his boots off he'd stand a little over six feet tall.

She placed his age somewhere in the early- to mid-thirties. His thick, dark brown hair was shaggy around the ears and hung to his collar in the back. As for his face, when he'd looked up at her, the blueness of his eyes had again grabbed and held her attention. Now, however, she noted that his nose was average and his cheekbones high. Beneath the heavy beard and mustache, she guessed he probably had a lantern jaw. Of course, she could be entirely wrong. Maybe he'd grown the beard to cover a weak chin. That, however, would be the only weak thing about him, she thought as he put his boots aside and rose.

She'd been concentrating on her inspection of him in an attempt to ignore the growing fear within her. But she could ignore it no longer. She was alone in an isolated cabin, in the midst of a blizzard, with a man she didn't know and a wolf who didn't seem all that friendly.

He took a step toward her, and she took a step back.

Peter frowned patronizingly. "Don't worry. I'm not a crazed backwoodsman who hasn't seen a woman in years. You don't have anything to fear from me."

She knew she didn't look her best. Her short brown hair was a wet stringy mess of curls. Her makeupless face was pale and drawn from strain causing her best feature—her dark brown eyes—to look sunken and overly large. Even at her best she was not a raving beauty, but she was pleasant enough looking. This man, however, made her feel like one of Cinderella's ugly stepsisters. *And I should be glad,* she told herself, quickly overcoming the sting of insult as she realized his disinterest was the key to her safety. "I'm glad to hear that." Her manner becoming businesslike, she held out her hand. "I'm Ellen Reese and I owe you a debt of gratitude."

"Peter Whitley," he replied, accepting the handshake.

Ellen had shaken hands with a great many men, but never had she been so aware of the contact. Her first impression was strength, then came the roughness of his work-callused palms. But the most disconcerting was the warmth. His hand was still cold from his recent trip outside, and yet a heat raced up her arm. Breaking the contact swiftly, she again took a step back.

His impatient frown returned. "You can have the bedroom. I'll take the loft."

"I don't want to put you out," she said, again feeling like an unwelcome intruder.

In spite of her bravado, Peter sensed her continued

fear. "The bedroom door has a lock on it. I figure you'll
feel safer in there. I wouldn't want to have you lying
awake all night worrying."

She was about to say she wouldn't worry, but the
words died in her throat. He sounded honestly disinter-
ested in her, but recent events warned her to distrust
what any man said. "Thanks." Not wanting to admit
that he was the entire reason she wanted the locked
door, she added, "I'm not so sure your friend's wolf
likes me."

Peter had to admit the animal could be intimidating.
He recalled the first evening he'd spent in the wolf's
company. No human had ever studied him so thoroughly. "He takes his time to decide how he feels about
people. But he won't hurt you. He'll accept my decision
to allow you to stay with us."

"That's encouraging," she said dryly, letting her
tone tell him she wasn't so certain she should take his
word for that. "Does he have a name?"

"Bane." The animal had risen and was now standing
by Peter. He looked up when his name was mentioned,
and Peter petted him fondly. "Jack Greenriver, the
owner of this cabin, found him when he was a pup. He
was wandering around the woods alone, nearly starved
to death. Jack figured his mother had been killed by a
mountain lion or hunters. He never found her den or
the rest of her brood. He brought Bane home and nursed
him back to health with the intention of releasing him
into the wild once he was strong enough. Jack even
taught Bane how to hunt so that he could survive on
his own, and he never gave him a name, just called him
wolf. But when he tried to send him back into the
woods, Bane continued to hang around the cabin. That's

when Jack started referring to him as the Bane of his existence. But the truth is, he'd grown as fond of Bane as Bane had of him, so they formed what Jack likes to refer to as an alliance, and Bane remained.''

Peter gave the wolf's head a playful rub. ''It's Bane you owe your life to. He's the one who realized some-one had turned into the drive and insisted on going out to investigate. When I heard him howling, I knew some-thing was wrong. Then I heard you honking.''

''Thanks,'' she addressed the wolf.

He tilted his head, and she had the feeling he was studying her, but he made no move toward her. After a moment he returned to his place by the hearth and, lay-ing his head on his paws, closed his eyes as if to say he was turning over the guarding of the cabin to Peter.

Peter picked up her suitcase and overnight bag and carried them into the bedroom. Returning to the living area, he headed to the refrigerator. ''How about some dinner? I was just getting ready to make corn bread and heat up some of the chili I made yesterday,'' he offered.

''Sounds good,'' she replied, suddenly realizing how hungry she was. ''What can I do to help?''

Keep your distance, was the response that flashed through Peter's mind. Like he'd told her, he wasn't a crazed backwoodsman, but he was only human, and she filled out that sweater and those jeans in all the right spots. ''I can handle getting dinner on the table on my own. Just make yourself comfortable.'' He motioned toward the study door. ''There's a phone in there. Feel free to make a call and let whoever is waiting for you know you're going to be delayed. If they're from around here, just tell them you're at Jack Greenriver's place. If not, say you're between Colebrook and West Stewardtown.''

"No one is expecting me." The minute the words were out she regretted them. Silently she berated herself for not making him think someone would be keeping an eye out for her. She studied his face for any clue that she'd made a gigantic mistake. What she saw was disbelief.

"This is not the kind of weather to be out for a Sunday drive in.''

"I had a destination,'' she returned in her defense.

"And where was that?''

"I'd promised myself I'd see Canada. I've never seen Canada.''

Suspicion spread over his face. She had that innocent, girl-next-door kind of look, but he'd been tricked before. "Are you running from the law?''

She scowled. "No." His gaze remained locked on her, and she had the feeling he wasn't certain if he should believe her. "It's a man. All right?" She'd meant to stop there, but the anger she'd been suppressing took control. "My fiancé, Charles. I didn't want to be in the same country with him.''

"You nearly got yourself frozen to death because of a lovers' quarrel?''

The "I can't believe anyone could be so stupid" look in his eyes grated on her nerves. But she couldn't fault him. "I'll admit I acted a bit rashly. I regret it. It certainly won't happen again. Now can we drop this subject?''

Whoever Charles was, he had a tiger by the tail with this one, Peter thought. "I've always made it a point to stay out of the middle of lovers' spats.''

Her scowl darkened. "This was a great deal more than a spat." Abruptly she clamped her mouth shut. She'd said enough. As she started toward the couch, a sudden worry came to mind. She'd called Paul Saunders, her supervisor, and explained that she needed to take a few vacation days effective immediately. She'd told him it was a family emergency. To her relief he hadn't asked any questions. He'd simply told her to take the time she needed. But she hadn't called her parents. They would have wanted an explanation, which she hadn't been ready to give. And she'd been in no mood to be diplomatically evasive. "I will take you up on the offer of the phone. Charles will probably think I ran home to Kansas City to my parents. He'll call them, and they'll worry. If you don't mind, I'll tell them I'm visiting a friend."

He gave a shrug of indifference and returned to making the corn bread. Out of the corner of his eye he caught the enticing little wiggle she had when she walked. A scowl spread over his face. She was already spoken for. Only a fool would consider getting involved with a woman who was in love with another man, and he was no fool.

Alone in the study, she made the call. Still unable to talk about the scene that had sent her on this insane drive, she simply reassured her parents that she was fine and that she just needed a few days away. After obtaining their word that they wouldn't reveal her whereabouts to anyone, she gave them the phone number for the cabin in case they needed to contact her.

"You're just having a little case of cold feet," her mother soothed. "It will pass. After all, you've been waiting a long time for the right man."

"I'm really not in the mood to talk right now," Ellen replied firmly, and said a quick goodbye before her mother could do any serious prying.

Wrapping her arms around herself, she stared out the window at the storm beyond. She'd lied; she didn't feel fine. Beneath her anger was the pain of betrayal, and it hurt worse than she'd ever imagined anything could hurt.

Chapter Two

Ellen dried the last pan and put it away. She'd insisted on cleaning up after dinner, partially because it was the polite thing to do and partially to keep busy. When they'd first sat down at the table, she'd prepared herself to discourage any further conversation about her private life. But she hadn't had to. Her host had been content to eat in silence. The extent of their verbal exchange had consisted of her complimenting him on the meal and him thanking her for the compliment.

Bane had eaten at the same time they had and now he was sleeping in front of the fire while Peter sat in a nearby chair reading. She'd noticed the book earlier. It was a massive tome about the Mayan civilization. He didn't exactly strike her as the scholarly type, but then she wasn't the best judge of men, she thought acidly.

"I noticed a large assortment of books in the study. Would it be all right if I chose one to read?" she asked.

"Consider yourself at home," Peter replied without

looking up from the page. He'd been trying to concentrate on a map of the ancient Mayan empire, especially that portion that had spread into Guatemala, but his unexpected guest had proved to be a distraction. He'd found himself covertly watching her and enjoying the view. Hopefully, she'd find a book, sit down and he'd be able to ignore her.

Bane lifted his head, looked disgruntled at having had his rest disturbed, then again laid his head down and went back to sleep.

Clearly, I'm the sort of woman who can't hold any male's attention, Ellen mused dryly, going into the study. A handsome, blue-eyed, blond-haired man's image filled her mind. Her stomach knotted and she felt sick. Pushing the image from her mind, she concentrated on the shelves of books. Most were nonfiction. Some were histories. The majority dealt with Native Americans. On closer inspection, she found that several pertaining to the healing arts practiced by the various Indian nations were written by Jack Greenriver. He'd also written one concerning the Eskimos. Choosing a book at random, she considered remaining in the study, but being alone made it too easy to remember what had sent her on this trek.

So far, her host and Bane had proved to be enough of a distraction to keep her mind off last night, and with any luck they would continue to be.

"You said this place belonged to Jack Greenriver?" she asked, returning to the living room.

Peter looked up. Her hair had dried into a mass of tiny ringlets. It looked cute, he thought, then frowned impatiently at himself. "Yes."

She got the distinct impression he didn't want to talk.

"I just wondered," she said crisply. "I found a shelf of books with that name as the author."

She's taken, Peter reminded himself curtly. "Jack wrote them. He's in Arizona visiting family and doing some research for a new book at the moment."

A blast of wind rattled the window in the kitchen area. "He's probably having a lot better weather there than we are here. Warmer, at least," she murmured.

Not any warmer than the heat she was kindling inside of him, Peter admitted silently. Apparently, he had been spending too much time alone. He returned his gaze to the page in front of him. "I suppose."

Again sensing that her host was not in the mood for conversation, Ellen told herself to keep quiet. She seated herself on the couch and began to read. But as interesting as the subject matter was, it could not hold her attention. Instead, she found herself covertly studying her host and comparing him to Charles.

Charles was thirty-five. She'd placed her host somewhere near that age. They were also near the same height and build. But they were clearly men of different ilks. Peter obviously did not make regular trips to the barber. She also guessed that the jeans and flannel shirt were his normal attire. Charles, on the other hand, had a standing weekly appointment with his hair stylist, and he never wore jeans. She tried to picture him in them but the image felt wrong. Denim didn't suit his personality. At work, he was always in a suit. At play, he wore designer slacks or shorts. He was a sophisticated, well-educated man with impeccable manners. But he wasn't a snob...just a louse.

She turned her attention back to her host. He'd displayed pleasant manners while they'd eaten. He hadn't belched or slurped. As for education, she knew he could read.

Peter had been attempting to ignore his guest. But her gaze was causing an uncomfortable prickling sensation. He cast an irritated scowl her way.

Quickly Ellen feigned intense interest in the page in front of her. But again her mind didn't focus on the words, instead the blue of her host's eyes intrigued her. Charles's eyes were blue as well, but they were more pale in color. Peter Whitley's eyes reminded her of sky darkened just before a storm.

Admitting that trying to relax was useless, she put the book aside, rose and went to the window to look out. In the dim light of the porch lamp she could see the huge flakes still falling, and the sound of the wind told her the storm was continuing to rage. "Shouldn't we call the nearest garage and make an appointment to have their wrecker come pull me out as soon as the storm subsides?" she asked, abruptly breaking the silence hanging over the room.

"I did that while you were washing the dishes," Peter replied.

She assumed that, like before, he would immediately return his attention to his book, but a prickling on her neck suggested otherwise. She turned and was met by a pair of cool blue eyes. "Thanks." That seemed, she thought, to be the major extent of her vocabulary since they'd met.

Hoping to rid himself of all temptation, Peter said, "If you're anxious to get out of here because you want to make amends with your fiancé, you could call him."

Her jaw tensed. "I can't talk to him. Not yet, anyway."

Her nervousness was making him edgy. Worse, though, was her moving around the room. He couldn't seem to keep his eyes off her. Deciding that, seated, she would be much less dangerous to his control, he said, "I apologize for not being a good host. If you'd like, we could play a game of chess or cards."

His offer, she could tell, was genuine, but the thought of sitting made her legs ache. "What I'd really like to do is scream."

"Go ahead. I'd be grateful for anything that would reduce the tension in this room."

That her distress was affecting him surprised her. She'd been sure her presence was no more noticeable to him than one of the chairs or some other inanimate object. "I'm sorry."

Peter found himself focusing on her lips and wondering how they would taste. He needed a diversion, something that would discourage such thoughts. Talking about her fiancé should do the trick. "I make it a rule never to pry into anyone else's private life. However, if it would be helpful for you to talk about whatever sent you on this excursion, I'm willing to listen."

The image of Charles wearing nothing but a bathrobe, caused Ellen's anger to rekindle. "Being a man, you'll probably think it's amusing."

He frowned at the implication that all men were insensitive clods. "I find nothing amusing about a person placing themself in danger."

Realizing she'd lashed out unfairly at him, she flushed. "I apologize. It's just that I trusted Charles. Now I'm wondering if I can trust any man."

"No one is perfect."

Too tense to remain in one place, she paced across

the room. Coming to a halt behind the couch, she met his gaze squarely. "I never expected perfection. And I was perfectly willing to forget about any liaisons he'd had before we started dating. But once he'd declared his love for me and we became engaged, I did expect fidelity." The anger in her eyes flared hotter. "Last night I caught him with another woman. I'm a mechanical engineer. He thought I was going to be at the plant all night working out a problem we were having with one of the robotic arms. But I solved it more quickly than I thought I would and stopped by his place with Chinese takeout. I figured we could have a late dinner together."

Peter found himself thinking that Charles must be a real idiot. "He was probably having one last fling before he marched down the aisle. Some men feel that need."

"You make it sound so frivolous, as if he'd done nothing worse than go out for a night with the guys." She studied him coldly. "Are you men so shallow you don't know the meaning of commitment?"

Again he bristled at being lumped into a single category with all other men. "*I* know the meaning of commitment. If I loved a woman, she wouldn't have to worry about me straying."

Ellen felt herself being drawn into the blue depths of his eyes. The purpose and resolve she saw there was so powerful it was akin to a physical force. Every instinct told her that this man meant what he said. As the blue of his eyes seemed to engulf her, the thought that he was what she'd waited all her life for flashed through her mind.

Peter was acutely aware of the way the brown of her

eyes was softening. *She's in a vulnerable state right now,* he reminded himself. It wouldn't be right to take advantage of her, and he'd always tried to do what was right. "Did you give him a chance to explain?" he asked curtly.

"Who? Explain...?" For a moment she'd forgotten about everyone and everything but her host. The intensity of the momentary, unexpected attraction she'd experienced shook her. His sudden aloofness suggested he'd been aware of her reaction and wasn't pleased. An embarrassed tint reddened her cheeks.

"Charles," Peter replied.

"Charles," she repeated the name. Her fiancé's image came sharply back to mind, and anger washed away her embarrassment. Her gaze became icy. "He tried to blame me. Can you believe that? He actually tried to blame me!"

"He tried to blame you for his affair?" *Interesting ploy,* Peter mused.

Her shoulders squared with dignity. "I suppose you'd consider me a throwback to another era, but I was saving myself for marriage." She caught the glint of surprise in his eyes. "Yes, that's right. Standing before you is a twenty-nine-year-old virgin. Bet you never thought you'd see one of those in this day and age."

"I never really gave it much thought one way or the other." Peter found himself thinking that she looked kind of cute when she was angry.

Her jaw tightened in proud defiance. "I figured it was a good path to follow. The consummation of my marriage would be special. In addition, I would also avoid the possibility of contracting AIDS and other undesirable diseases or ending up pregnant out of wedlock."

Her anger flared hotter. "And it hasn't been easy. I'm not frigid. There have been times when I was tempted."

Peter saw the flicker of hurt that passed over her features and knew that behind her anger was the pain of someone who felt betrayed. "A lot of people would consider your decision admirable."

"If so, they're keeping awfully quiet," she retorted, pacing once again. "Newspapers, television and magazines have the soap box, and the majority of what I read and see wouldn't support your view." She breathed a tired sigh. Again approaching the couch, she rested her hands on its back and faced Peter levelly. "But then I've never let what anyone else thought determine my course of action. Even after we became engaged I insisted on waiting until our wedding night. I thought it would make the consummation of our love more important somehow."

The bitter edge returned to her voice. "He claimed it simply made him frustrated. He said he was a healthy male and needed female companionship. He said it was my fault he had to seek out a different companion." She straightened, indignation etching into her features. "And do you know who he chose? No, of course you don't. Well, I'll tell you. It was the twenty-two-year-old redheaded receptionist from the plant. I'd seen her flirting with Charles, but I trusted him."

Peter found himself not liking the role, but he heard himself playing the devil's advocate. "There is another way to look at this."

She glared at him. "And what way is that?"

"Maybe he's gotten his cheating out of his system. Better now than after the vows are said."

"I can't believe you're defending him! Do you men always stick so close together?"

Peter frowned. "I'm not defending him. I just think that since you obviously care a great deal for him, you should consider all the possibilities."

"*Cared.* Past tense," she corrected.

How much he wanted to believe her, stunned him. *If you do, you're a fool,* he warned himself. "If you don't still care, then why are you so upset?" he asked.

"Because I feel humiliated! Duped! Made a fool of!"

He wasn't convinced. "I think you should relax and get some sleep. Once you're rested, you'll be able to think clearer."

Ellen stared into the fire. "Maybe I don't want to think clearer. My mother didn't say so, but I know she's worried I'll never find anyone to marry if I don't marry Charles, and maybe that same fear is lurking down deep inside of me. It might convince me to overlook Charles's indiscretion, even if I'm not totally convinced he would remain faithful once we were married." Her jaw tensed. "I don't want to be married to a man I can't trust."

"It could be that he'll realize how much he cares for you and never stray again," Peter said.

Ellen breathed a tired sigh. "Maybe." Having revealed a great deal more about herself than she'd wanted to, she fell silent.

The man would be a fool if he didn't, Peter thought. Sensing their conversation had reached its end, he returned his attention to his book. This time, telling himself that his guest was still in love with her fiancé and therefore totally off-limits to any further lustful

thoughts, he ordered himself to concentrate on his research.

Rounding the couch, Ellen sat down and stared into
the fire. Bane had woken during the exchange between
her and Peter. Now, out of the corner of her eye, she
saw that he'd gone back to sleep. That he'd shown no
reaction to her display of anger caused her to realize
that the wolf had accepted her as a nonthreatening en-
tity. That, at least, was a relief.

Still, she remained tense as, uninvited, her host's image filled her mind. She recalled her sudden, very
strong, totally surprising attraction for the bearded man.
Obviously she was experiencing some sort of rebound
reflex, she decided. She'd never thought of herself as
the kind of woman whose emotions could bounce so
radically, but then, she'd had a shock, catching Charles
with Janet and been terrified, thinking that she might
freeze to death or be eaten by wolves. It was only natural her emotions were a little out of control.

Also, she had to admit that Peter wasn't bad looking
in a caveman sort of way. On top of that, he'd saved
her life. It was only natural, she'd feel a certain affinity
toward him. *Just don't go thinking what you're feeling
is anything more than gratitude,* she warned herself.
She had enough trouble ahead, sorting out her feelings
about Charles. She didn't need to confuse the issue with
a rebound attraction to a stranger.

Having had this little talk with herself and confident
she had her emotions reined in, she still found herself
being curious about her host. "What do you do when
you aren't cabin- and wolf-sitting for a friend?"

Silently Peter groaned. He'd been trying to ignore

her, but it was obvious she wasn't going to make that easy. He looked up.

She read the impatience in his eyes and felt like a nuisance. "Never mind," she said with apology. "It's none of my business."

He knew he'd behaved impolitely. But she was a strain on his control. "I travel a lot. I'm a geologist. I go where my work and interests take me," he informed her, then returned his attention to his book, letting her know he considered this exchange over.

And you're not inclined to talk about yourself, she added mentally. Respecting his right to privacy, she closed her eyes and leaned her head back on the couch. The image of her and her host climbing a mountain together began to play through her mind. Scowling, she opened her eyes and glared at the wall above the mantel. Her emotions were in turmoil, and now her mind was traveling absurd paths! Peter was right. She needed some sleep.

"I'm going to bed," she announced, abruptly rising. "Good night and thank you for your hospitality."

Peter read and stoked the fire while he waited for his guest to settle in for the night. It wasn't until she'd finished in the bathroom, entered the bedroom and closed the door that he relaxed.

Reaching down, he scratched Bane's neck. "Jack always says you have a nose for trouble. He's right. The sooner we send Miss Reese on her way, the better."

After closing and locking the bedroom door, Ellen climbed into the bed. From the next room she could hear her host muttering something and guessed he was

ELIZABETH AUGUST   35

talking to the wolf. *He's probably making a joke about
my stupidity,* she mused. She couldn't fault him. She
had behaved stupidly. If she'd wanted to cross a border,
she should have headed for Mexico.

The wind buffeted the cabin. As she snuggled farther
under the fluffy down comforter, the phrase "snug as a
bug in a rug" ran through her head. Clearly she was
still in shock from the discovery of Charles with Janet.
She was a prisoner of the storm, trapped in a cabin,
seemingly in the middle of nowhere, with a stranger and
a wolf for companions. There should be nothing comforting or snug about that.

Too tired to ponder this curious course of emotions,
she closed her eyes and immediately drifted to sleep.

Chapter Three

Ellen woke to the smell of bacon frying. Recalling that she'd not only told her host the embarrassing details of her breakup with Charles, she'd even told him about her mother's fear of her becoming a spinster, she groaned and buried her face in the pillow. The thought of hiding out in the bedroom for a while longer appealed to her. Unfortunately hunger and the call of nature thwarted that plan. Dressing quickly, she ran a brush through her hair. The thick mass of brown tresses had a touch of natural curl and were cut into a short, easily managed style. Usually, she wet any wayward strands then blow-dried them into submission. This morning she ignored the fact that one side was flattened, while a patch of hair toward the back of the top wanted to stick out. She also opted to forgo any makeup.

Impressing her host was not at the top of her list of priorities. Getting her car unstuck and heading back to Boston was.

"Morning," she said as she left her room and walked briskly to the bathroom.

"Morning," Peter returned, keeping his back to her and continuing to watch the food he was preparing.

His tone was polite but cool, and Ellen had the distinct feeling that the sooner she was gone, the better he'd like it. *Two minds that travel the same path,* she mused, entering the bathroom.

"Hope you like pancakes," he said when she came out a few minutes later. Without waiting for a response, he set a plate with a stack of three, along with several strips of bacon, on the table at the place she'd occupied the night before. "If you want more, help yourself. There's more batter in the refrigerator," he added, heading to the door. "The snow has stopped and the weather is supposed to remain clear for the next few days. I'm going to go see about your car."

She looked at the pancakes and her mouth watered. But pride rebelled at allowing him to do all the work. "I want to come along." Abruptly, her stomach grumbled loudly in protest.

He paused in the act of pulling on his coat. Until now, he'd purposely avoided looking at her. She'd drifted in and out of his dreams last night, each time running back to a shadowy figure named Charles. Both his conscious and his subconscious minds were warning him to stay clear of her, and he intended to do just that.

But manners refused to allow him to continue averting his gaze. Turning to her, he didn't think he'd ever seen eyes so dark brown or a woman who looked so deliciously disheveled. He scowled impatiently at himself. *Keep your mind on business,* he ordered.

As Ellen headed to the rack of coats, her stomach growled loudly, protesting once again.

Getting her on her way as quickly as possible was a priority, but he didn't want her fainting from hunger. "You eat. I need to move more wood onto the porch before I head out to your car."

She was certain he was changing his plans to accommodate her, but she was too hungry to argue. "I won't take long," she promised, already retracing her steps to the table.

As she gobbled down the pancakes, she wondered if they were as good as they tasted or if she was simply so hungry anything would appeal to her. Coming to the last couple of bites, she decided that they were truly excellent. And the bacon had been perfectly prepared as well. Peter Whitley, she concluded, would make a great husband. Unexpectedly she found herself wondering what it would feel like to be in his arms. "My cooking is just fine," she declared, telling herself that she didn't need lights of fancy clouding her mind. She was confused enough as it was.

The sound of wood being stacked reminded her she was slowing her host's efforts to get rid of her. Rising as she forked the last bite into her mouth, she carried her dishes to the sink, rinsed them, then again headed toward the coatrack. Halfway there she recalled the icy wind that had entered the cabin when he'd gone out and paused to make a side trip to the bedroom. There she pulled on a sweater over the turtleneck and shirt she was already wearing and a second set of socks, then hurried to join him.

Seeing her, Peter dumped the load of wood he was carrying on the pile at the end of the porch and motioned for her to follow him. ''The way this snow drifts, we'll probably have to shovel some before Jasper can even find your car,'' he said, explaining why two shovels were strapped to the side of the snowmobile.

She nodded, waited for him to seat himself, then climbed aboard. As the uneven terrain forced her to hold more tightly to him, and the cold wind caused her to huddle against his back, she found herself thinking she'd never known a more sturdy man. In her mind's eye she recalled how he'd looked without his bulky coat...the broadness of his shoulders, his flat abdomen, the sturdy columns of his legs.

She couldn't believe the very close-to-lecherous path her thoughts were taking. It had to be some kind of rebound reaction, she reasoned. Having wanton thoughts about an almost complete stranger wasn't like her. The moment the machine was stopped, she released him and dismounted.

Peter drew a breath of relief. Halfway to the car, he'd begun undressing her, imagining how her soft curves would feel in his hands. Clearly he'd been without female companionship far too long, he mocked himself. Unstrapping the shovels, he focused on the business at hand.

Bane circled the vehicle then ran off into the woods pursuing his own interests while Ellen examined the drift that had built around the front and passenger side of the car. On the passenger side, it formed a snowbank that continued to a good foot above the roof of the car. As soon as Peter finished unstrapping the shovels, she took one and began to free the vehicle.

''Tom Grady keeps the drive plowed,'' he said as they worked. ''I've told him to come and clear it as far as your car to make it easier for Jasper to pull you out. But he won't be able to get around your vehicle. He'll have to come back to do the rest once you're gone."

Again she heard impatience in his voice. "I'm really sorry to be such an inconvenience," she said tersely. "I can dig out my car on my own. Why don't you run along and take care of whatever chores you need to take care of."

Peter frowned. She disturbed his peace of mind, but that didn't make it right for him to make her feel unwelcome. "I didn't mean to sound as if you were a nuisance." He told himself that her business was her business and to say no more, but he couldn't stop himself. "I just hope you think twice before you take off in a snit again. Next time you might not be so lucky."

That he'd felt he had to remind her of her stupidity grated on her nerves. "I've learned my lesson. So could we please drop the subject?"

Hearing the hostility in her voice, he mentally kicked himself for not keeping quiet. After all, he wasn't her keeper. "Consider it dropped."

Ellen nodded and concentrated on freeing her car.

They had it nearly dug out when a heavy duty, four-wheel-drive police car came to a stop at the end of the drive. "Morning," the uniformed officer called out, leaving his vehicle on the main road, its hazard lights flashing to warn any motorists of its presence, as he climbed out and made his way toward them.

"Morning," Peter called back, setting his shovel aside and walking to meet the man.

Wanting to ask about the condition of the main road to the south, Ellen also set her shovel aside and approached the policeman. He looked to be in his late forties, she decided, and about five feet ten inches tall without his wide-brimmed hat.

"Peter Whitley?" The officer held out his hand as the two men reached each other. "I'm Rick Mack."

"Jack has mentioned you. Says you're an excellent tracker," Peter said, accepting the handshake.

The office grinned. "That's a real compliment coming from Jack." Bane came running up at that moment, not stopping until he'd reached Rick. "Morning, Bane." The policeman gave the wolf a friendly rub on the head. Bane accepted the greeting, then took a stance to one side as the policeman looked to Ellen. "I don't believe we've met."

"Ellen Reese," she said.

"Ms. Reese." The officer touched his fingers to the rim of his hat in a polite salute.

She saw the hint of interest in his eyes and knew he was guessing that she was an intimate friend of Peter's, but she didn't care. All she wanted was to be on her way back to Boston. But before she could ask him about the roads, he turned toward Peter.

"Jack Greenriver said we could count on your help in any rescue that might come up. There's a plane down somewhere in these woods. A four-seater. Husband, wife, three-year-old son and one-year-old daughter on board. They took off this morning as soon as the storm had passed. The husband called in an SOS about an hour later. Transmission went dead in mid-sentence. The homing device must have been damaged in the crash because we aren't getting any signal. If you and Bane could scout the area east and north of Jack's cabin, I'd be grateful. We've got choppers flying overhead, but there's a lot of forest to cover."

"Count me in," Peter replied.

Her own problems were forgotten as fear for the family in the downed plane swept through Ellen. "I'd like to volunteer, as well."

Apparently the woman hadn't learned her lesson about going off half-cocked, Peter thought dryly. "You don't know these mountains. We could end up having to rescue you."

"He's right." The policeman smiled politely at her. "I appreciate the offer, but it'd be best to leave this up to those who know what they're doing." He handed a walkie-talkie to Peter. "If you find anything, give me a call." Having completed that bit of business, he looked toward Ellen's vehicle. "Jasper said you'd put in a call for a wrecker."

"Miss Reese didn't realize how bad our weather could get up here," Peter said in an easy drawl.

Ellen fought back another wave of hostility as the policeman gave him one of those good-ole-boy "women ain't got no common sense when it comes to staying out of trouble" looks. "Since I can't be of assistance here, I'll head back to Boston as soon I can get my car onto the main road," she said keeping her voice level.

Rick Mack's expression became apologetic. "The roads are still in bad shape. Even four-wheel-drive vehicles are having a difficult time of it. We're advising people to stay put for a day or so. Besides, Jasper's helping with the search. He told me to tell you it'd be a while, tomorrow at the earliest, before he could get here."

Hating the idea of imposing on Peter Whitley for

even another minute, Ellen asked, "Is there any way I could get to a hotel or motel?"

The policeman glanced toward Peter, a frown beginning to form and suspicion entering his eyes.

"Mr. Whitley has been a perfect gentleman. And I greatly appreciate him giving me shelter for the night." Ellen spoke up quickly, not wanting to get Peter into any trouble. "It's just that I hate imposing on him further."

The policeman's expression relaxed. "I'm afraid you're going to have to. According to the latest reports, all of the local hotels and motels are fully booked." Obviously eager to resume the search, he again extended his hand to Peter. "Good luck. Even if any of the people in the plane survived the crash, if we don't find them soon, they'll freeze to death."

"Bane and I will start looking immediately," Peter promised accepting the parting handshake.

The officer nodded his thanks and headed back to his vehicle.

"I'll drop you off at the cabin," Peter told Ellen as he collected the shovels and strapped them to the snowmobile.

She knew he would think she was a hindrance but she refused to sit idly. "I'm coming with you. I know a little first aid."

He started to insist that she remain at the cabin. He didn't need her distracting him. But he knew if he did find survivors, he could use help. Besides, he didn't have time to argue, and she looked determined. If he left her behind, she might set out on her own. "Fine. We'll stop by the cabin and pick up some blankets and a medical kit."

Turning to Bane, he pointed in the direction of the area he'd been asked to cover and said, "Search."

Immediately the wolf took off at a loping run.

"Jack taught him that the command search means to look for people in need of help. If he finds them, he'll come back and lead us to them. His nose is worth a dozen pairs of eyes," Peter explained as they mounted the snowmobile. Then he started the engine, cutting off any further conversation.

A short while later, they'd gotten rid of the shovels, picked up the blankets and first aid kit and were making their way through the woods. The rough terrain and abundance of trees made the going slow. Periodically Peter stopped the snowmobile, turned off the motor, listened, called out, then listened again. When they received no response, they continued.

The winter wind was bitter, and even Ellen's heavy clothing was not a total protection against it. Her legs felt icy and her hands were cold beneath warm covering. But she thought of the two small children, and fear for them made her forget her own discomfort.

Suddenly Bane appeared, coming at a run from the north. He yapped, saw that he had Peter's attention, then turned to retrace his steps.

"Keep your fingers crossed he's found them," Peter yelled to her as he followed the wolf. "They can't last much longer in this cold."

"I'd cross my toes as well if I could," she yelled back.

What seemed like forever, but was only a few minutes later, they entered a clearing. At the far end was a small plane, its wings sheared off and the body wedged between the trees.

"Looks like the major portion of the body's intact," Peter noted as they sped across the small clearing. "That's a hopeful sign."

Reaching the plane, he shut off the snowmobile and began talking into the walkie-talkie. Ellen could see how the helicopter, if it had passed over this area, could have missed spotting the wreckage. The skid path across the clearing looked like a shallow ravine. Only a very small portion of the plane's tail would have been visible from the air and even that might be hidden by some of the higher branches, depending on the angle at which the chopper would have flown over.

Bane howled, and from inside, Ellen heard the cry of a child. Grabbing the blankets, she hurried to what was left of the cabin while Peter gave their location to the other rescuers. Opening the door, she climbed inside. The two children were still strapped into their seats by special safety harnesses. The windows had miraculously stayed intact. Still the interior of the plane was frigid and the smallest child looked blue around the lips and was slouching lifelessly.

The mother was limp against the back of her seat. A trail of blood from her head had seeped into the fabric of her heavy sheepskin coat. The father was draped over the control panel.

The oldest child looked up at her. "Help?" he asked hopefully.

"Yes, help," she replied, fighting back the threat of tears.

Taking only enough time to cover him securely with a blanket, she turned her attention to the second child. Pressing her cheek against the little girl's, she held her breath hoping to feel some sign of life. She was not certain if it was wishful thinking or real, but she thought she detected a tiny whimper. Lifting her head away, she looked at the small, soft-featured face. Nothing. Praying they were not too late, she freed the baby, wrapped the child in a second blanket, then opening her coat, held the little girl against herself, hoping to share her own body warmth.

Peter had entered the plane and was checking the mother. "She's still alive," he said, wrapping another blanket around the woman. He looked up at Ellen. "How's the little one?"

She was again pressing her face against the child's cheeks trying to detect any signs of life. A second tiny whimper reached her ears. "She's alive," she said around the lump in her throat. "But my guess is just barely."

"Help us?" the boy asked again.

Ellen knelt beside him, gently squeezing his hand in hers. "There's lots more people on the way."

He wasn't paying any attention to her. Instead, he was looking at his mother. "Mommy's hurt." Then his gaze shifted to the pilot's chair. "Daddy, too."

"We're doing everything we can," she replied, not wanting to lie to him.

"The father's still breathing, but it's very shallow," Peter said, covering him with a blanket as well. "Stay in here. I'm going into the clearing and keep an eye out for the rescue teams. The chopper should be here any minute."

"Let's hope it gets here real quick," Ellen returned.

"Real quick," he seconded, and left.

From outside Ellen heard Peter praising Bane for a job well done, then ordering the animal to go home.

Continuing to hold the child tightly to her, she freed one hand and tucked the blanket more securely around the boy. Then for added warmth, she pulled her coat as much around herself and the little girl as possible.

Battling her fear that help would not arrive in time, she noticed the strain of shock on the boy's face. Attempting to soothe him, she asked his name.

"Philip," he replied. He looked toward the bundle in her arms. "Clara. My sister."

She smiled encouragingly. "I'm pleased to meet you, Philip. I'm Ellen and the man outside is Peter."

"Ellen," he repeated. "Get help?" he asked again.

"Yes," she assured him.

The sound of the helicopter brought a relieved smile to her face. "Sounds like it's arriving now. We'll have you, your sister and your parents on the way to a hospital in no time."

He nodded solemnly. "Hospital. Help."

She gently stroked his jaw. "Everything's going to be all right." As her words echoed in her ears, she hoped she was right.

From outside, she heard men's voices, then the door was opened and a medic entered. The next few minutes were hectic. The chopper was too small for two stretchers, the children and the medics. Since the children could be transported as they were and the sooner they were in a hospital, the better, it was decided that Ellen and Peter would accompany them in the chopper while the rest of the team remained behind to get the husband and wife out of the plane and ready to be transported when the second chopper arrived.

As the chopper headed upward, Ellen clutched the little girl to her. Other than the two faint whimpers and some very shallow breathing, she'd detected no other signs of life, and the worried looks on the medics' faces had increased her concern. Trying to think positive thoughts, she glanced toward Peter who was holding the boy on his lap. There was a gentleness in the man's eyes as he gave Philip an encouraging smile and wink, and she found herself thinking that the man looked very natural with the child.

A crew of people in white coats pushing two gurneys came running toward the helicopter as it landed on the pad by the hospital. Knowing that the children were finally someplace where they could be treated, Ellen breathed a sigh of relief as she handed the little girl to a nurse.

Suddenly a microphone was being pushed in her face.

"What condition are the children in?" a tall redhead demanded.

"They're alive. The boy seems in pretty good shape. I don't know about the little girl." Suddenly realizing she was speaking into a camera, she clamped her mouth shut.

"What about the mother and father?" the redhead persisted.

Not wanting to say anything more, Ellen backed away, easing behind Peter, using him as a shield.

"I'm going back to the crash site," the pilot informed them. "You two getting out or going back with me?"

"Going back. The sooner the better," Peter replied, before Ellen had a chance to answer. He'd had his share of publicity and learned to dislike it. In his opinion, it only brought trouble to a person's doorstep. "Get back," he yelled at the reporter and camera crew. "We're taking off."

Relieved to be free of the reporter and her crew, Ellen returned to her seat. Slowly a tear trickled down her cheek as the fear she'd been holding back took over. It was followed by another and then another. Brushing at them, she looked to Peter. "Do you think the little girl will survive?"

"Where there's life there's hope. Children are resilient." She looked so worried he wanted to wrap his arms around her to reassure her, but he didn't trust himself to keep his actions strictly brotherly. He settled for giving her hand a squeeze. "You did what you could." Seeing that her coat was still open and her seat belt unfastened, he leaned over, closed the coat and fastened the belt.

It was a simple act, done in a businesslike manner, yet to Ellen it seemed intimate somehow. Even more, this show of protectiveness caused a warm glow to spread through her. Silently she groaned. Her reactions to this burly man were greatly exaggerated.

Peter sat back in his seat and shoved his hands into his pockets. All he'd done was fasten her coat and seat belt, but even that had felt much too personal. Trying not to think about his companion, he recalled the reporter and the camera and frowned. He'd let Ellen hide behind him giving the camera a good shot of him. The frown deepened. Reaching up, he stroked his beard. Surely with his face so obscured by whiskers, his anonymity would be protected.

Abruptly he grinned at himself. He was last year's news...no, he was last decade's news, he corrected. It had been several years since anyone had poked a mi-

crophone in his face. Besides, even if someone remembered him, he'd learned how to protect his privacy. His
jaw tensed. He'd also learned how not to be easily de-
ceived by people...women in particular.

Chapter Four

As she ate her sandwich, Ellen tried to concentrate on the logs blazing in the fireplace rather than her companion. She and Peter were back at the cabin. After the helicopter had returned them to the crash site, they'd stayed long enough to talk to some of the rescuers and had discovered that, although their conditions were critical, the husband and wife had been alive when they'd been transported to the hospital. Assured they could be of no more assistance, they'd retrieved Peter's snowmobile and headed home. Now, exhausted, with night falling outside, they sat in front of the fire eating.

"I'm sorry I have to impose on you for another night," she said, breaking the silence between them.

"It's not an imposition." *But it's definitely a strain on my nerves,* he added to himself.

She again stared into the fire. The images of the children and their parents haunted her. Peter had called the hospital but hadn't been able to find out anything definitive. "I wonder how Philip and Clara and their parents are doing."

Peter had been recalling the fear in the little boy's eyes and wished he could have done more. But only the doctors could help right now. "It's about time for the nightly news, maybe that reporter has found out something. She was pushy enough."

He clearly didn't like the press, Ellen noted. But then that would be natural for a man who coveted his privacy as much as Peter Whitley coveted his.

Peter crossed the room and opened a tall, wide, wooden cabinet.

Surprise registered on Ellen's face when she saw the television inside. She'd assumed the cabinet housed guns or blankets and clothes. When he mentioned getting information from the nightly news, she'd thought he was going to retrieve an ancient radio or maybe even contact someone on the ham radio outfit in the study.

"I would have asked last night if you wanted to watch television, but storms always interfere with the reception, and I knew none of the stations would be coming in. But we should be able to get something tonight," he said as picked up the remote, switched the screen on and returned to his chair.

They caught the redheaded reporter in mid-sentence while the camera was on Ellen handing Clara over to the nurse. Suddenly the camera was doing a closeup on Ellen. Looking pale and drained, she heard herself speaking into the microphone.

To Peter's relief, although the station ran the footage of him as Ellen moved behind him, his beard and mustache did obscure his features, and the reporter gave no names, identifying them only as the couple who had found the plane. Then came footage of the husband and wife arriving at the hospital.

They were John and Brenda Pyress, the reporter informed her audience. John was an out-of-work pilot on his way to Canada to start up a bush pilot business with his brother. "A miracle on the mountain. An angel must have been looking after the young family," the reporter proclaimed, then went on to say that Philip, the son, was doing well. He'd sustained only a bruise or two and the little girl, although she'd experienced some hypothermia seemed to be doing very well, and the doctors expected a full recovery. The mother and father were both listed in critical condition but were expected to survive.

Tears welled in Ellen's eyes. "Thank goodness."

Peter nodded. "They were lucky."

As the realization that she'd helped save four lives sank in, Ellen experienced a sense of elation like none she'd ever felt before. She grinned at her two stoic companions. "Come on guys, admit it. We make a great team."

Bane looked lazily up at Peter as if this was old stuff to him and he didn't understand her exuberance.

Peter, however, wasn't paying any attention to the animal. Instead, he was captivated by the excitement on her face. Her happiness was bringing him a surprising amount of pleasure. "Yes, we do," he heard himself admit.

Ellen's grin broadened further and she met his gaze. Suddenly she was caught in blue depths that reminded her of a summer sky. The television became nothing more than a droning in the distance. Her host held her attention with a magnetism so strong it was as if they were physically touching.

For Peter, the urge to cup her face in his hands and taste her lips was close to overwhelming. He reminded himself of his rule to play it slow and careful with any woman. And this one, his inner voice cautioned, most of all. She was on the rebound. But the temptation to pay no heed was winning.

Suddenly the cabin seemed to vibrate, the windows rattled and Bane was on his feet, alert for action. From outside, the roar of a motor grew intense, and light flooded the clearing. The moment was gone. *And a good thing, too,* Peter told himself, rising and striding to the door.

Ellen gasped. The feeling of having had something very special ripped away jarred her. Then it was forgotten as she, too, headed to the door to find out what was going on.

A small helicopter had landed in the clearing surrounding the cabin. The searchlights that had helped the pilot see his way down were still on, illumining the night. As Ellen and Peter stepped out onto the porch, they saw the woman reporter from the hospital alighting along with a cameraman. She yelled up at the pilot, and he turned off his engine.

"The plane crash has caught the imagination of the country," the woman explained, hurrying toward them. "The powers that be who decide what stories get top billing liked 'the miracle on the mountain and the angel on their shoulders' theme. People want to see the couple who found them. And the wolf. When the local police told us you had a wolf helping you, my producer went wild."

"We're not interested in any publicity," Peter said, starting back into the cabin.

Ellen was already ahead of him, having eased herself further and further back out of view as the woman and cameraman approached. She'd come up here to hide out, not to be on television.

But before Peter could close the door, the reporter had placed herself on the threshold. "You don't know all the trouble I had to go through to get here. Your drive is blocked and we had to find a helicopter that could land here. And surely you don't want to rob people of a happy news story," she pleaded.

"I'm sure if you show them pictures of children, that will give your story all the warmth it needs," Ellen spoke up.

"Look, I won't use your names," the redhead bargained.

"Going live in thirty seconds," the man with the camera announced.

"The top brass was so excited they sent down special equipment," the reporter persisted. "National," she added pointedly. "Look, all you have to do is tell how it felt to reach the plane and find the family alive." Abruptly she grinned.

Following the direction of her gaze, Ellen saw that Bane had taken a stance beside Peter.

"Key in on the wolf," the reporter ordered her cameraman.

"Live in ten, nine, eight, seven, six, five, four, three, two, one, you're on," he said aiming the lens at Bane.

"I'm Sally Wynman here in the northernmost reaches of New Hampshire," the woman said, "where today a miraculous rescue took place. The rescuers...a man, a woman and their wolf." She shoved the microphone into Peter's face. "According to reports I received, the two of you are here on vacation and volunteered to help with the rescue. You'll have quite a story to tell the folks back home."

Ellen shifted uncomfortably. The reporter had made it sound as if she and Peter were a couple. She wanted to correct that impression but could think of nothing that wouldn't make the situation worse.

Peter simply glared.

"According to my source, it was your wolf that found the wreckage and led you to it," the reporter hurried on when she realized she wasn't going to get any response.

"Yes," Peter said curtly, his manner threatening her to ask him any more questions.

She gave him an "I've been threatened by meaner men than you" look and continued to face him. "How did you feel when you entered what was left of the plane and discovered the family was still alive?"

Cursing silently at the redhead's determination, Peter saw his opportunity and took it. "Ellen was the one who entered the plane first."

Immediately Ellen had the microphone shoved into her face. "What were you thinking?"

Seeing no way out but to respond, Ellen said, "I was both relieved and scared for them. It was very cold."

"What did you..."

"We're breaking up," the cameraman warned. "We're down." He grinned. "But they liked what we got."

"Get off this property now, or I'll call the police and have you arrested for trespassing," Peter ordered.

Bane snarled, and the reporter and cameraman backed toward the door. He took a step toward them and they hurried out onto the porch.

"All I want is a little more of an interview to play later," the woman pleaded.

"You've got all you're getting," Peter growled and slammed the door in their faces.

Ellen shivered. With the door open so long, the cold air had pervaded the cabin.

Scowling at the news anchor on the television promising more about the rescue later, Peter snapped off the set, then threw a few more logs on the fire. While he and Ellen stood near the flames to warm themselves, the reporter banged on the door several more times, but after getting no response, she and her crew left.

Silence had once again descended over the cabin when the phone rang. Peter answered, intending to threaten the reporter with a harassment suit if she was the caller. The woman's voice on the other end faltered when he issued his curt hello, and he realized he'd scared whoever it was.

There was a sharp intake of breath, then the caller said tersely, "I want to speak to my daughter, Ellen Reese."

"It's for you." He held the receiver out to Ellen. "I believe I made a very bad first impression on your mother."

"Your dad and I saw you on television." Her mother's anxious tones came over the line the moment Ellen said hello. "You never mentioned a wolf and who was that man? He sounded dangerous."

"He's not. He's a friend, and the wolf is a pet."

"The reporter made it sound as if you and your friend were a couple...as if you were living together."

Ellen heard the question in her mother's voice. "We're not having an intimate relationship. Mr. Whitley offered me shelter when my car got stuck in the snow. I knew you wouldn't approve, so I didn't mention that I was staying with a man."

The anxiousness in Ruth Reese's voice increased. "He not only sounded ferocious, he looked ferocious the way he glared at that reporter. Are you sure you're safe there?"

"He's been a complete gentleman."

"Well, you are twenty-nine years old. I should be able to trust your judgment by now."

Ellen frowned at the continued doubt in her mother's voice. "You can."

"But what if Charles saw the broadcast? He's already called here three times looking for you. What shall I tell him if he calls and demands to know who that man was?"

"Just tell him I'd never met Peter Whitley until I arrived here in New Hampshire and that we both just happened to volunteer for the rescue."

"I intend to continue to let Charles believe that the friend you're staying with is a woman. I don't see any reason to totally destroy any future you two might have together simply because you got cold feet and did something foolish."

Ellen scowled into the receiver. "I'm not the one who put mine and Charles's relationship at risk." The sensation of being watched caused her to glance over her shoulder and see Peter looking her way.

Immediately he turned his attention back to the fire,

but his mind remained on Ellen. She'd used the term "put at risk," which meant she hadn't made up her mind to dump this Charles person she was engaged to. Mentally he patted himself on the back for keeping his distance. She was irate and felt betrayed, but he was sure she still loved the guy.

A heavy sigh came over the line. "I'm sorry, dear," Ruth said. "I didn't mean to sound critical. It's just that I think you and Charles make such a lovely couple. You seem so well suited to each other. And he is a wonderful catch."

Except that I can't trust him, Ellen thought bitterly. Aloud, she merely said, "Sometimes appearances are deceiving."

"Just don't do anything rash. Your father and I had our share of lovers' quarrels before we married. If we'd let a silly little misunderstanding come between us, you would never have been born."

"I promise you I will think things through thoroughly. I always do."

"You have always had a level head on your shoulders," Ruth conceded, the doubt still lingering in her voice. Suddenly, she said, "Your father wants to talk to you."

Ellen grimaced. Her mother always put her father on the phone when she thought Ellen wasn't listening to her and might do something irrational.

"Hi, sweetheart," David Reese's voice came over the line almost immediately.

She heard the concern in his tone and frowned. "Really, Dad. You don't have to worry about me. I'm fine."

"Yes, of course you are," he soothed patronizingly.

"It's just that your mother and I want what's best for you."

Again Ellen had the feeling she was being watched. Glancing out of the corner of her eye, she saw both Bane and Peter looking her way. Bane had his head tilted slightly sideways as if he didn't understand what the problem was. Peter was frowning, and she wondered if he was worried that he might find himself the groom in a shotgun wedding.

"I want what's best for me, too," she replied.

Peter found himself wondering if Charles really was the best for her. *That's not my business. She's a big girl. She can take care of herself,* he told himself and forced his gaze back to the fire.

"Charles is a fine young man," David Reese said.

"Charles isn't perfect," Ellen snapped back.

"None of us are."

She knew he was honestly concerned about her welfare, but he was talking to her as if she was a child. "I assure you that I've got the situation under control. Now I want you and Mom to stop worrying. I'll call you when I get back to Boston."

"Just remember that we're always here for you," he persisted.

"I know that and I appreciate it," she replied, then added firmly, "Good night, Dad," and hung up.

Peter had intended to make no comments about the phone call. They were strangers...ships passing in the night. The less he involved himself in her problems, the better. But instead of remaining silent, he heard himself saying, "Sounded as if your parents were a little upset about you being here with me."

"You definitely didn't make a good first impression," Ellen agreed. Recalling her mother's mention of his inhospitable manner toward the newswoman, she grinned. "You didn't intimidate the reporter, but you certainly did my mother. In fact, I'll bet the majority of women in the television audience are wondering how I put up with you."

He cocked an eyebrow wryly.

Her grin vanished, and she gave herself a mental shake. For one brief moment she'd actually pictured herself as his girlfriend, defending him to those women.

"Should I expect your parents to come rescue you?" he asked grimly, the thought causing a disquieting image of two middle-aged adults pounding on his door, self-righteous indignation on their faces.

Sinking onto the couch, she gave him a dry look. "No."

"Glad to hear that." Peter told himself to drop the subject. Ellen Reese's private life was none of his business. She would be gone, probably by tomorrow, and he'd never see her again. No doubt she'd forgive Charles, marry him, raise a family and live happily ever after. This scenario was supposed to ease his mind. Instead it irritated him. "I got the impression they were worried about Charles seeing the news report."

Ellen pushed herself further back into the couch and scowled at the fire. "Apparently they're both worried that Charles might be my last chance at finding a husband. I guess my mother told my father about the statistics regarding educated women my age finding a mate, and the percentage didn't look encouraging."

"What about you? Are you worried enough to marry a heel?" Inwardly he frowned at himself. That had come close to sounding as if he was trying to talk her out of marrying Charles.

Her gaze leveled on him. "No. But do I want a husband and a family, and I thought Charles was the perfect match for me. He's kind, romantic and considerate." Her gaze returned to the fire, and a grimace of uncertainty skewed her features. "But he's also human. Maybe I'm being too judgmental. Maybe in a moment of weakness he felt the need to have a final fling." She recalled the instances of unexpected attraction she'd been experiencing toward the host. "We all have our moments of irrational weakness."

"Sounds like you're still in love with the guy and searching for a reason to forgive him." He'd been certain this was the case, but he didn't feel like congratulating himself for being right. Instead an uneasiness wove through him. *I just don't want to see her make a mistake that will bring her unhappiness,* he reasoned. After all, he'd saved her life. In some cultures that would make him responsible for her.

"Maybe." Exhaustion threatened to overwhelm her. She didn't want to discuss Charles, her parents or her chances of finding someone else any longer. She pushed herself to her feet. "I'm tired. Good night."

Miss Ellen Reese and her love life were not his concern, Peter again told himself sternly, and picked up the book he'd been reading the night before. Still, he could not put her entirely out of his mind. The uncertainty he'd seen in her eyes bothered him. *She's in love with Charles, so forget her,* he grumbled at himself.

A few minutes later Ellen climbed into bed. As she closed her eyes, an image of Charles entered her mind.

Grudgingly she admitted that she was a little worried about how he would react if he saw her on the news. Well, he, of all people, had no right to be judgmental!

Ellen woke with a throbbing headache. The blackness outside the window told her it was still night. Switching on the lamp on the bedside table, she read the clock: 3:00 a.m. *Go back to sleep,* she ordered herself. But the throbbing grew worse.

Leaving the bed, she retrieved the bottle of aspirin from her overnight case, pulled on her robe and opened the bedroom door. Peter had left the light on in the bathroom and the door ajar just enough to allow her to find her way across the central living area. Pausing in the kitchen, she found a glass, then went into the bathroom and closed the door before running any water.

After swallowing down the pills and using the facilities, she took a look at herself in the mirror. "I look like something the wolf dragged in," she jested, noting the dark circles under her eyes.

Hoping the aspirin would work, she started back to the bedroom.

"Are you all right?" Peter's voice broke the stillness.

Startled, she jerked around to discover him at the foot of the ladder leading up to the loft. He was wearing only a pair of jeans, and a curl of heat wove through her. She didn't think she'd ever seen a man who looked more virile. "I just woke with a headache."

"Do you need some aspirin?"

The impatience in his voice made her again feel like a nuisance. "I had some. I'm sorry I disturbed your sleep."

Mentally Peter kicked himself. He'd sounded inhospitable, but he was fighting a strong surge of arousal. The desire to pull her into his embrace, feel her soft curves against him, was making his blood race. He'd definitely been spending too much time alone. "I'm the one who should be apologizing. I can be a bear when I first wake up."

Bear was a good description, she thought, her gaze traveling over his bearded face to the dark curly vee of hair on his chest. The temperature of her blood seemed to rise, and she found herself wondering how it would feel to run her hands over his chest, then into his thick, nearly shoulder-length hair. "I can be a little grouchy myself." She'd meant to sound polite but indifferent. Instead, there was a husky edge to her voice.

Even as he ordered himself to go back to bed, Peter moved closer. "An Eskimo healer Jack introduced me to taught me how to rub the back of my neck to relieve a headache. It usually works."

Ellen told herself to say good-night and go back to bed. Ignoring the order, she stood rooted, her breath locked in her lungs in anticipation. She wanted him to touch her. "Maybe you could demonstrate."

He warned himself he was treading on dangerous ground, but he couldn't stop himself. "I suppose I could." Circling around behind her, he began to massage the taut muscles of her neck and shoulders.

Ellen wanted to purr. "That feels incredibly good."

Feeling her muscles relaxing, Peter told himself to stop, but her body was too enticing. He worked his way along her shoulders, then back to her neck.

"You should have been a healer," she murmured.

As she leaned into his hands, he worked his way lower.

When he reached her waist, Ellen commanded herself to step away from him. But her legs refused to function. He moved closer, his chest pressing against her back. The heat of the contact pervaded her and desire flamed to life as his hands massaged her hips then continued to her thighs. When he leaned forward for a longer reach, his beard tickled her neck while his arms encased her. "You've cured my headache," she said, marveling that the words had come out coherently.

"I'm glad I could help." He waited for her to move away. When she didn't, he told himself that he should. Instead, he pictured her legs wrapped around him, and his hands moved upward, seeking to explore her curves more fully. Through the fabric of her robe, he cupped her breasts.

A sultry moan of delight escaped from deep in her throat. Lost in a daze of sensation, Ellen slowly moved against him, massaging his body with a catlike motion. He felt so sturdy.

Peter trailed the tip of his tongue from the hollow of her ear down the cord of her neck. She tasted delicious. Hearing something that sounded very much like a purr, he smiled and let his hands travel downward again, this time seeking more intimate regions.

Ellen's breathing became ragged and she parted her legs to allow him access. Her whole body was on fire now. Pressed against him, she could feel his manhood coming to full arousal. She reminded herself of her vow of celibacy until marriage. *What's good for the goose is good for the gander,* a little voice argued.

Her breathing, the way she continued to remain pliable beneath his touch told Peter of her willingness. He pictured himself carrying her to the bed. The word *vir-*

gin suddenly flashed into his mind. For a moment the lust-aroused male animal in him reveled at the thought of being the first man to possess her. Then a chill of reality swept over him. Did he really want that responsibility? She'd waited a long time for Mr. Right. He couldn't take her in a moment of weakness. She'd hate him afterward and then there was the guilt he'd have to live with knowing he'd taken something from her he could never give back.

Placing his hands on her shoulders, he stepped back, then released her completely. ''I told you that you were safe here. And I'm a man of my word. You came here a virgin. You'll leave as one.'' Before she had time to respond, he was on his way back to the loft. *That was definitely the hardest thing I've ever done,* he admitted as he climbed the ladder. And he knew he would never have the strength to do it again. One of them would not be spending tomorrow night in this cabin. If he had to, he'd ride the snowmobile over to Tom's place and bunk there.

For a long moment Ellen stood immobile. A wave of frustration at having been deserted was quickly followed by shock and disbelief. After all these years of insisting on waiting for her wedding night, she'd been on the verge of giving herself wantonly to a nearly total stranger. She needed to get back to Boston, back to familiar territory where she could think clearly. Tomorrow she'd be on her way, even if she had to leave her car behind and hitchhike home.

Striding to the bedroom, she closed and locked the door, then stood leaning against it. She was grateful to Peter but appalled and embarrassed by her own behavior. What shook her even more was how natural being touched by him had felt.

"I've heard that rebounds can be intense," she murmured. "Obviously that's what this was."

Still, as she crawled under the covers, the lingering feel of his hands taunted her. *I just got caught up in a romantic fantasy,* she reasoned. Sequestered with a handsome stranger...strike the *handsome,* she corrected. She wasn't really certain what he looked like, with that facial hair obscuring his features. However, his nose was nice and those eyes of his were captivating. Then there were his lips...soft and warm...and his beard and mustache had felt so incredibly enticing as they'd brushed her skin. A tremor of desire shook her.

"Stop that!" she growled at her body.

She returned to her original line of thought. Sequestered with a stranger and a wolf in a picturesque cabin in the woods. Add to that the excitement of having been involved in a rescue. And, of course, there was her continued anger toward Charles. It was no wonder her emotions and therefore her reactions to everything and everyone were heightened.

Punching her pillow, hoping to make it more comfortable, she told herself to go to sleep. She had a long day ahead of her. With her escape from this cabin the only thought in her mind, she once again slept.

Joining Peter at the table for breakfast the next morning, Ellen told herself not to bring up their early-hours encounter. Peter had made no mention of it. He had, in fact, appeared to have forgotten all about it. But her behavior was a source of embarrassment that nagged at her.

"I want to thank you for not taking advantage of me," she said stiffly. "I'm not wanton. I honestly don't understand what happened."

Peter hadn't slept well after returning to bed. He'd dreamed about her and woken feeling agitated. He had to work to keep his tone casual. "I figure you're still mad enough at Charles to want to hurt him, and what better way than to have an affair of your own."

"I suppose." She grimaced ruefully. "But that's a rather destructive approach. I've never thought of myself as being masochistic." An embarrassed flush darkened her cheeks. "I didn't mean that as an insult. Having an affair with you wouldn't have been masochistic...except that I'd have been doing it for the wrong reasons."

"And you would have hated yourself afterward and probably despised me, to boot." Peter repeated his own reasoning for having stopped before they'd done something they both would have regretted.

Ellen breathed a relieved sigh. "I appreciate you being so understanding." Allowing the subject to drop, she began to eat.

Peter also ate, but he didn't feel understanding. What he felt was frustrated. As soon as she was on her way and he'd taken care of some business that needed his attention, he was going into town. There was a good-looking, dark-haired waitress by the name of Linda at the café who'd been giving him inviting looks for the past couple of weeks. Today he'd flirt back and ask her for a date.

Chapter Five

"You look like a man with a lot on his mind."

Peter glanced up from his coffee to see Linda standing beside his table looking down at him with friendly concern. Two hours earlier, he and Jasper had gotten Ellen Reese back on the main road. As soon as she was on her way to Boston, he'd taken care of some business, then headed into town. But instead of pursuing the pretty waitress, he'd been sitting there thinking about his recent houseguest. "I'm worried about a friend," he replied.

Linda smiled sympathetically. "If you want to talk, I'm not real busy right now."

He looked around to discover he was the only customer left in the place. "There's not much to talk about."

She eyed him narrowly. "It's a woman, isn't it. The one you were on television with?"

"She's none of my concern," he growled, the same words he'd been repeating over and over to himself.

"Got it bad, huh?" Linda breathed a disappointed sigh and eased onto the bench on the other side of the booth. "I'm sorry to hear that. I've been thinking you might be just the man I've been looking for, but you're obviously taken."

Peter scowled into his cup of coffee. Only a fool would fall for a woman who was in love with another man—and he was no fool. "It's not that kind of relationship. I saved her life. Now I feel responsible for her. She might not be thinking too clearly at the moment."

Linda gave his hand a squeeze. "We all have to make our own mistakes. Believe me, I know. My first husband was in love with the bottle. I thought I could change him. I couldn't. My second had a roving eye. I couldn't cure him, either. Both times my mother warned me that I'd be sorry, but I knew I'd always wonder if she was wrong and I'd passed up my Mr. Right. In the end I followed my instincts." She laughed lightly. "Obviously they aren't very good. But I've had enough good times to outweigh the bad. That's what keeps me looking."

Peter's jaw hardened. "You're right. She's an adult. She should make her own decisions."

"When you get ready to burn that bridge you're standing on, let me know. Maybe I can help you forget her," Linda offered, rising to wait on a customer who'd just entered.

"Yeah, thanks," he replied absently. He was picturing Ellen returning to Boston, patching up her differences with Charles and marrying him. The image left a bitter taste in his mouth. What if the guy was a heel? What if he strayed after the vows had been said?

That's her problem, he grumbled to himself. But he

couldn't make himself totally believe that. Like it or not, he felt responsible for her. Maybe he should go to Boston and have a look at this Charles. Ellen had suggested her parents might be enamored of him because they saw him as her last chance for a husband. As an impartial bystander, Peter argued, he'd be able to make a more accurate judgment of the man.

"And so ends my adventure," Ellen announced under her breath, exiting the hospital. She'd stopped to see how the children and their parents were doing since their rescue, before continuing on to Boston. To her relief, the doctors were already discussing when the children could be released, and the adults were expected to recover, as well. Both sets of the children's grandparents had arrived and were spoiling the boy and girl royally, but Ellen figured they deserved it after what they'd been through.

She'd also learned from the desk nurse that only moments before her arrival, a good Samaritan, who insisted on remaining anonymous, had called to say he was buying Mr. Pyress a new plane so he and his brother could go on with their plans to set up their own business.

"Now it's time for me to return to the life I left a couple of days ago," she finished, reaching her car and climbing in. The realization of how little time had passed since she'd left Boston stunned her. Well, a lot had happened. Peter's face entered her mind. He'd looked relieved to see her go. "Bet our paths never cross again," she muttered dryly, pulling onto the main road and heading south.

By the time Ellen arrived at her apartment, she was exhausted. During portions of the drive, the road conditions had worsened, and she'd had to concentrate totally on driving. Those times had been the best. Whenever her mind had been able to wander, she'd relived Charles's courtship. He'd been charming and persistent. But always her mind had flashed back to the night she'd found him with Janet, and her anger was as fresh and as strong as ever.

Entering her apartment, she saw the light on her answering machine blinking. Dropping her suitcase and overnight bag on the living room floor, she pressed the button and sank into the soft oversize chair by the couch.

"Ellen, we have to talk," Charles's voice issued from the tape. "I love you. I know you probably don't believe that, but I'm not perfect. I gave in to a moment of weakness. Please, don't let my stupidity ruin our future together. I'll do anything to make it up to you."

That message clicked off and another clicked on. This time it was her mother. "Charles called here looking for you. He wouldn't tell me what happened, but I know something is wrong. Please call and let me know you're all right."

Ellen silently congratulated herself for having called her mother from Peter's cabin. She hadn't meant to worry her parents.

The next four messages were from Charles—all begging her to give him a chance to explain.

Leaning back in the chair, she stared out the sliding glass doors that gave access to her balcony. The stars looked farther away here than they had in New Hampshire, and smaller. Her apartment also felt curiously empty. Peter's presence did fill a room, she admitted.

Actually, more accurately, it had filled the entire cabin. And then there was Bane.

She frowned. Surely she wasn't missing them. They certainly weren't missing her. Her frown deepened. She was only thinking of them, she told herself, to evade the real issue...what to do about Charles. Forcing her bearded rescuer and the wolf from her mind, she turned her head just enough so that she could see her telephone.

Should she call Charles right now? It was late. A musing expression spread over her face. If a woman answered, she wouldn't have to make any decision about taking him back. Forcing herself to her feet, she crossed the room, picked up the receiver and dialed his number. He answered on the third ring.

She tried to speak, but her anger had returned locking her vocal cords. Dropping the receiver into its cradle, she grabbed up her bags and went into her bedroom. On the dresser was the five-carat diamond engagement ring he'd given her. She'd been too stunned, seeing Janet come down the stairs barely covered in one of his shirts asking if the food had arrived and saying she was famished by all the exercise he'd provided, to do anything but turn and flee. Halfway back to her apartment, she'd noticed the ring still on her finger. She'd ripped it off at the next stop sign. The urge to return and throw it at Charles had been strong, but she hadn't wanted to see him again just yet, so she'd left it on her dresser when she'd left town.

The thought of touching it caused her stomach to churn. Tonight she'd get some sleep. Tomorrow she'd face Charles.

* * *

The next morning Ellen chose the gray, pin-striped, tailored suit she wore when she was giving important formal presentations at work and waited until she was fully clothed, including makeup and high heels, before placing the call to Charles's office. He wouldn't be able to see her, but for some reason she'd never fully understood, she felt more in control when she was wearing what she termed her "battle" clothes.

"Ellen?" Harriet Masters, Charles's secretary, asked, relief evident in her voice. "I'm so glad to hear your voice. Charles has been a bear the past couple of days. I don't know what you two fought about, but I do hope you patch things up."

"Is Charles available?" Ellen asked noncommittally.

"For you, yes. Hold on just one second."

Ellen heard a buzzing, then Charles's voice came over the line. "Ellen. Are you back in town?"

Again anger threatened to freeze her vocal cords. She scowled at herself and they unfroze. "Yes."

"I'll be over in a few minutes."

She wanted to meet on neutral ground. "No," she blurted, but it was too late. He'd already hung up. Dropping the receiver into the cradle, she drew a deep breath. Neutral ground wouldn't have worked, anyway. There would have been other people around, and she didn't want an audience.

Going into the bedroom, she picked up the engagement ring, put it in its box and carried it into the living room. There she paced the floor until she heard his knock.

"Look, I know what I did was wrong," he said the moment she opened the door.

She wanted to shove the small jeweler's box into his

hand and slam the door in his face, but before she could act, he'd brushed past her and entered. Closing the door, she turned to face him. "I don't think I can ever trust you again."

"Of course you can." He took her hand in his. "Everyone has moments of weakness and makes mistakes. I've had mine. I know the consequences. I would never risk losing you again."

He sounded sincere, and the plea in his eyes looked genuine. She felt herself wavering. "I suppose that is one way of thinking about it."

A scowl suddenly darkened his brow. "Besides, I, at least, kept my liaison private. You were on national news."

She'd been wondering if he'd seen the broadcast. Now she had her answer. And either he hadn't spoken to her parents afterward or he hadn't believed them.

"I blame myself for anything rash you did," he continued curtly. "But did you have pick such a lowlife?"

Ellen's back stiffened defensively. "Nothing happened between us. *And* Peter is not a lowlife!"

"All right. A hick, then. I really thought you had more sophisticated taste. The man lives with a wolf and looks as if he's never been off that mountain. Of course, I guess you weren't in the mood for conversation." An edge of accusation entered Charles's voice. "If you'd been more like that with me, none of this would have ever happened."

"Nothing happened," she repeated.

He didn't look convinced. "Your parents said you were visiting a friend. How long have you known him?"

She caught a flash of jealousy in his eyes and it

brought a twinge of pleasure. "I lied to my parents the first time I spoke to them because I knew they would worry. I met Peter Whitley Sunday night when he rescued me from freezing to death. He considers my presence in his life a nuisance."

Charles's features relaxed somewhat signaling that he was beginning to believe her denial of having had a tryst. "And absolutely nothing happened?"

The memory of her and Peter's late-night encounter returned. "Nothing of any consequence."

Charles scowled. "I knew it. He made a pass at you."

"No, he didn't." She would never term what had happened between them a pass. Besides, she was as much to blame as Peter. And, she recalled, he'd been the one who had stopped them before they'd both done something they would have regretted. "We mixed like oil and water." Having had enough of being on the defensive, she added caustically, "Unlike you and Janet."

Guilt spread over Charles's features. "I swear nothing like that will happen again." He raked a hand through his hair. "Look, we've both behaved stupidly." Catching the fire in her eyes, he added quickly, "Me, most of all. But let's not let this destroy us."

Ellen was tempted to forgive him. He looked so stricken. Then the scene from Saturday night again played through her mind. "I can't marry a man I can't trust." She picked up the jeweler's box lying on the table and extended it toward him.

He took a step back. "No. I won't believe it's over for us. You keep the ring. You don't have to wear it if you don't want to, but you keep it and give me a chance to prove I can be the husband you want."

Ellen stood mutely, torn about what to do.

He drew near again and stroked her jaw. "Love isn't something that dies easily. I know you still care for me. Otherwise you wouldn't be so hurt and angry. I'm going to win you back."

Before she could respond, he was gone.

Standing, watching the door close behind him, she sighed tiredly. If he was being honest about being faithful, then she should forgive him. Her hand went up to her cheek. His touch had once made her feel warm and cozy. Now all she wanted was to wipe away any lingering sensation. Forgiving him was going to take some time.

Suddenly the door opened and Charles stuck his head inside. He grinned boyishly. "Oh, and by the way, I told my parents that the man in the cabin...you said his name is Peter Whitley?" He paused to allow her to respond.

"Yes," she confirmed.

His grin returned. "I played dumb on the name. I told them you'd mentioned it to me, but I couldn't remember. It wouldn't have washed for us to be giving out two different names. Anyway, I told them that he's your cousin. That's also what all the people at the plant believe. I figured that would save you from some embarrassing explanations. I couldn't bear the thought of your reputation being ruined because of me. And I do blame myself for everything." With a conspiratorial wink, he again departed.

A part of her said that she should be grateful. Another part pointed out that she wasn't the only one being saved from embarrassment. Charles would have had to put up with people whispering behind his back about his fiancée having an affair. And not just any common, ordinary affair, but one with a mountain man who lived with a wolf.

"You're becoming cynical," she berated herself. Most men, even under similar circumstances, wouldn't have been so understanding as Charles. She toyed with the jeweler's box as she carried it back into the bedroom, recalling how excited she'd been the night he'd given it to her.

Standing in front of her dresser, she opened it and, staring down at the ring inside, tried to recapture the joy of that moment. Instead she felt the ache of betrayal.

A knock on her door caused her to jump. Putting the ring box on the dresser, she answered the summons. It was a florist with a huge bouquet of pink roses.

The card read:

"I love you, and I'm willing to start from the beginning once again if that's what it takes to win you back. Love, Charles."

She recalled that their courtship had begun with a bouquet of pink roses. In that instance, too, they had been sent as an apology. As vice president of Tucker, Inc., it was Charles's job to see that production and quality was maintained at a level to satisfy their buyers. That morning he'd called her into his office to rake her over the coals for a recurring problem with one of the robotic mechanisms that was setting the schedule behind. As it turned out, the problem hadn't been her fault. He'd sent the roses and arrived right behind them with a caterer who provided a gourmet dinner, including the candles, fine china and silverware.

Tears brimmed in her eyes. He'd swept her off her feet. She'd thought they were the perfect couple. She'd thought he was perfect.

"No one is perfect," she chided herself. Scowling at her naiveté, she breathed in the fragrant scent of one of the blooms. Was she judging Charles too harshly? After all, he'd been willing to forgive her.

"Mom has told me many times, a successful marriage requires forgiveness and compromise," she reminded herself.

Peter knocked on the door of the tall, brick town house belonging to Professor Ian Cochran. Ian's field was archaeology...a subject Peter not only found fascinating but useful in his work. As a student, he'd sought the professor out to discuss the routes ancient people had chosen to travel, seeking not only food and shelter but also the ores and gemstones they valued. Their long discussions had led to a close friendship.

Ian, white-haired, slender, looking spry for his seventy-plus years, answered and greeted him with a laugh and a hug. "You're a sight for sore eyes. Come in. The coffee is brewing, and I've got a fire blazing."

"I appreciate the favor," Peter said, following his host into the living room.

"Now tell me what this is all about. You said you needed an excuse to be in Boston." Ian's eyes were filled with interest. "I hope it involves a woman. You can't let one bad experience spoil you for all time."

"It does involve a woman, but it's not what you're thinking." Without mentioning his lusty attraction or their early-morning encounter, he told Ian about Ellen Reese.

"So she was the woman with you at the cabin. She seemed nice." Ian nodded approvingly. Then he grinned. "And now you're having second thoughts about sending her back to her fiancé."

"Only because I don't want to see her make a mistake she'll regret. I feel responsible for her. But I don't want her getting the wrong idea and thinking I'm some lovesick fool who chased her here. That's why, if anyone asks, I need you to tell them that you called me and invited me down for a few days to discuss some research you're involved in."

Ian continued to grin. "Of course."

Peter frowned sternly. "This is strictly platonic. I just don't like the idea of sending her right back into the same situation that caused her to endanger herself in the first place."

Ian raised a skeptical eyebrow.

"As soon as I'm satisfied she's behaving rationally, I'm on my way to Guatemala," Peter finished, determined to make it clear that he meant what he said.

"No matter how interesting you find your work, it can't replace a warm, loving body next to yours at night," Ian stated sagely.

Peter scowled. "You said something about coffee."

"Yes." Levering himself out of his chair, Ian led the way to the kitchen. "I do hope I get to meet this woman you feel so *responsible* for."

Not if I have anything to say about it, Peter retorted mentally. He didn't want Ian planting false notions in Ellen's head. Aloud, he said, "I doubt you will."

The old professor sighed. "Too bad."

Ellen frowned indecisively. Tomorrow she would go back to work, and there was one person she was truly dreading seeing…Janet.

"I have two options," she reasoned aloud. "I can either find a way to accept her presence or quit." Quitting just because she didn't want to face Janet was cowardly. And waiting until tomorrow for their encounter since seeing the redhead in Charles's apartment was grating too much on her already taut nerves.

"Better to take a bitter pill quickly." She shoved herself out of her chair and to her feet. A few minutes later she was driving to the plant. She would stop by her office on the pretext of picking up some work she'd left behind and wanted to look over before tomorrow.

Entering the gate she smiled at the security guard, made a noncommittal remark when he mentioned he'd seen her and her cousin on television and continued to the main facility. Passing through the double glass doors, she braced herself. But Janet wasn't at the reception desk. Instead, an efficient looking woman with graying hair glanced up and smiled as Ellen passed by.

Ellen forced a returning smile. Feeling as if she would look like an idiot if she simply turned and left, she continued to her office. Janet probably wasn't any more interested in encountering her than she was in encountering the redhead, she surmised, guessing the receptionist had called in sick. A curl of pride wove through her. At least she'd had the courage to confront the situation rather than hide in her apartment.

"Hi." Marilyn McMurphy called out, approaching from the other end of the hall. Marilyn, thirty-seven, a little on the plump side, married with two children, was Paul Saunders's secretary. Reaching Ellen, she stopped. "Mr. Saunders said you had a family emergency." Interest sparked in her eyes. "I suppose it had something to do with that cousin in the mountains?"

"His father was ill and wanted to see me," Ellen lied. What difference would one more fib make, she reasoned. And hers made it sound as if she hadn't been alone with Peter.

Sympathy showed on Marilyn's face. "I hope he's better."

"Not much," Ellen replied. Then, wanting to turn the conversation away from her exploits, she said, "I just came by for a minute today. Tomorrow I'll be officially back. Will you tell Paul that for me?"

"Be happy to." Marilyn leaned closer to Ellen and lowered her voice. "Did you notice our new receptionist?"

"As a matter of fact, I did," Ellen replied, fighting to keep her tone level. She didn't want to show too much interest.

"She's only temporary, but Janet's not coming back."

Relief swept through Ellen, and she allowed her curiosity to show. "Really?"

"According to Alice in personnel, she called in Monday morning, said she was using her vacation time as her notice time and resigning."

An uneasiness replaced Ellen's relief. Had Charles given the receptionist the option of resigning or being fired? If so that wasn't fair. He was as much to blame as Janet for what had happened.

"And, as far as I'm concerned, she won't be missed," Marilyn continued. "She was always flirting with the men—married, single, young...old. She didn't seem to care. If you ask me, she was trouble looking for a place to happen."

And she found it, Ellen added silently.

Marilyn's condemning manner again changed to one of curiosity. "It must have been exciting rescuing those people."

"It was exhilarating to find them alive," Ellen admitted.

"Your cousin looked a bit ferocious, but I suppose I'd have been upset having my privacy invaded by a bunch of reporters, especially if I was worried about an ill father on top of everything else."

"He's not fond of people arriving uninvited," Ellen replied, recalling the impatience she'd seen on Peter's face as he and Jasper had worked to free her car so that she could be on her way. Not wanting to discuss him further, she smiled apologetically and added a sense of urgency to her voice. "I've really got to run."

"See you tomorrow," Marilyn called out to her departing back.

By the time Ellen reached her office, she was again questioning her vision of Charles. She'd thought he was the kind of man who would be faithful. She'd been proven wrong. However, in all fairness, she again pointed out to herself, he was only human, and Marilyn was right about Janet being a persistent flirt. Even more, Charles appeared to be truly repentant.

Still, she couldn't help wondering if there was another side to his character, a darker side, she had not yet seen. In addition to being unfaithful, had Charles used Janet and then cast her aside like unwanted trash? Her uneasiness grew.

Punching in the extension for personnel, she asked

for Janet's address, claiming the woman had been very helpful to her and saying she wanted to write her a thank-you note. A few minutes later she was on her way to the address they'd given her. It was an apartment complex not far from the plant. Turning into the parking lot, she saw Janet putting a potted plant into a car, and Ellen pulled into the empty space next to it.

As Ellen climbed out of her car, Janet closed her car door and turned to face her. "Look, what happened between Charles and me was just a one-time thing. It didn't mean anything to either of us."

"That's a very generous attitude for someone who just lost her job," Ellen said dryly.

Janet regarded her ruefully. "Look, I know you're angry with Charles, but you should consider yourself lucky. He's a real gentleman. If you're thinking he tossed me out on my ear, you're wrong."

Ellen was again recalling seeing Janet coming down the stairs wearing one of Charles's shirts. Not wanting to look at the woman any longer, she shifted her gaze to the interior of the car. The back seat was filled with boxes as well as an assortment of plants. "You appear to be moving." A thought occurred to her, and she again looked the redhead in the eyes. "Has Charles decided to set you up in a little love nest I'm not supposed to discover?"

Janet frowned. "No. The man honestly loves you. After you left, he didn't say a word to me. He just got dressed and went after you. I figured I shouldn't wait around, so I came home. The next day he came to see me. I figured he'd tell me that he would see that I never got another job in this town and he wanted me gone by sundown. But he didn't. He was real polite and offered to help me get another job. He told me that he wanted you back and that he figured he had a better chance of you forgiving him if I wasn't around as a constant reminder of his indiscretion. I told him that I didn't like the winters here and wanted to go to California, so he wrote me a check to help get me there and get me started again.''

Janet's manner became one of a person dispensing worldly advice. "Look, for what it's worth, in my opinion you should forget last Saturday night ever happened. You've got a guy who's rich, handsome, generous and he loves you. Now if you don't mind, I've got to finish packing and head west before my plants freeze.''

Ellen said nothing as she climbed back into her car. Driving away, she recalled how despondent Charles had looked when he'd caught up with her at her apartment. A scowl darkened her features. That was when he'd tried to place some of the blame for his actions on her. Infuriated, she'd thrown him out and ordered him to leave her alone. But he hadn't left. He had continued to knock on her door until one of the neighbors had threatened to call the police. Then he'd found a phone and called her. He tried to apologize, but she'd been too upset to listen. She'd hung up on him in midsentence. He'd called back several times and each time she'd hung up the moment she'd heard his voice. In the end, she'd taken her phone off the hook.

And now he'd bought off his playmate, sent her packing so she wouldn't be a constant source of strain.

"He does appear to be doing everything he can to win me back,'' she conceded. But the fairy-tale "happily ever after'' feeling was gone and could never be revived. Again she scoffed at herself. "Happily ever after'' without any hurts or rough spots was an adolescent, unrealistic attitude. As harmonious as their relationship had been until Saturday night, she'd known that eventually they would run into a few bumps. She just hadn't expected infidelity to be one of them.

She breathed a tired sigh and again wondered if she was being too judgmental. Charles had been willing to forgive her when he thought she'd rebounded into Peter's arms. Besides, if he had learned his lesson, this could be a good thing. They weren't married yet, so technically he hadn't actually forsaken their vows.

And she could understand how he'd stumbled. Her temptation to surrender to desire in Peter's bed was still vivid in her mind. Even now, she could almost feel his hands caressing her. A tremble rippled through her as the passion he'd awakened was rekindled.

The car behind her honked, making her aware that the light had turned to green.

Stepping on the gas, she tried to recall a time when Charles had aroused her so spontaneously or so intensely. There weren't any. He'd awakened desire, but nothing so overpowering she'd felt out of control. But then, she'd never been this confused or this on edge. It was merely jumbled nerves that had caused her reaction to Peter Whitley's touch.

"And he is out of my life. What I need to decide is if Charles should be, as well," she grumbled at herself.

Chapter Six

Deciding she'd waged enough battles for one day, Ellen changed into jeans and a sweatshirt, made herself a sandwich and plopped down in front of the television. The roses Charles had sent were on the coffee table, but she chose to ignore them. After clicking through the channels a couple of times, she settled for watching a rerun of an old detective series.

She was swallowing the fourth bite of her sandwich when a knock sounded on her door. For a long moment she considered pretending she wasn't at home. The knock sounded again.

Shoving herself to her feet, she approached and looked out the peephole. A young man with two huge bouquets of roses, one red and one yellow, was standing there.

"Miss Ellen Reese?" he asked, when she opened the door.

"Yes."

Relief showed on his face. "I've been trying to deliver these all morning." He twisted so that one of the vases was within her grasp.

Accepting it, she allowed him to follow her inside with the other. Now with three bouquets on her coffee table it looked like a garden.

"I'll be right back," the deliveryman said and hurried out.

Frowning in confusion, she returned to her door to see him hurrying down the hall to the steps leading to the outside door. A couple of minutes later he returned with two more vases, one with white roses and the other with an elegant arrangement featuring a magnificent stem of orchids. Those, she had him put on her dining room table.

"I hope that's it," she said.

"For now," he replied cryptically, and left.

Ellen read the first card, then the second, third and fourth. They were all from Charles. Each mentioned one of their more memorable dates, and each vowed to win her back.

She had to admit that he was definitely serious about their relationship. And they had had some very good times together. He'd made her feel very special. Still, instead of enjoying this plethora of flowers and having her doubts eased by his obvious remorse, she continued to feel uneasy and restless.

Her jaw tensed. It was time to talk to her mother. Hitting the mute button for the television, she picked up the phone. When Ruth Reese answered, Ellen told her mother why she'd taken off for New Hampshire on the spur of the moment.

"And Charles swears he will never stray again?" Ruth asked when she'd finished.

"Yes."

"My mother would say 'Once a philanderer always a philanderer,' but I'm not so sure that's true. Although no one ever talked about it the way they do today, I have the impression that even in mine and your father's younger days, a lot of men had one last fling before walking down the aisle. Now, I'm not saying that your father did. But I do recall hearing a few suggestive remarks about your uncle's activities the night before his wedding."

"If Dad had strayed and you'd known about it, would you still have married him?"

Ruth was silent for a long moment, then said, "I think so. I loved him very much."

"So you think I'm judging Charles too harshly?"

"I think you need to decide if he's truly repentant and will settle down and be a faithful husband, or if this is a sign of trouble ahead. But keep in mind that men have stronger sex drives than women, and you *were* insisting on waiting until the marriage."

Ellen glared at the silent action on the television screen. "Charles tried to use that same argument. However, there are a lot of studies that show women to have just as strong a sex drive as men."

"Now don't get angry," Ruth soothed quickly. "I didn't mean to imply that it was your fault this happened. I admire you for going against current trends. Your father and I are both very proud of you for sticking to your values. I'm just saying you need to take all the factors into account. Charles is, after all, merely a man. He is, however, a very good catch, and you two were so in love.''

Hanging up a few minutes later, Ellen continued to let the television run on mute as the events of New Year's Eve played through her mind. She and Charles had been at a party at his parents' home. It was a large estate on the outskirts of Boston. Everyone was dressed in their best finery. The chandeliers sparkled and the champagne flowed. There was a string quartet in the parlor for those who preferred sedate tones, while a small band in the ballroom played a mixture of big band, rock and roll and current favorites.

A knock on her door startled her, jerking her back to the present. Thinking it might be Charles, she considered not answering, then frowned at herself. Hiding from him was not going to solve her dilemma.

As she opened the door, her eyes rounded in surprise. ''How did you find me?'' she blurted, staring up into Peter Whitley's bearded face.

He frowned indulgently. ''You're in the phone book.''

Ellen continued to have a hard time believing this was really happening. Of all the people she'd ever met, he was the last one she'd expected on her doorstep. ''More to the point, why are you here?'' she asked in calmer tones.

''I'm in town on business and thought I'd drop by and make certain you got back all right.''

She'd expected him to look out of place and uncomfortable in the city. Instead, he was his usual intimidating self. ''Well, as you can see, I did.''

His gaze raked over her. Same tempting curves. He shouldn't have come. ''So I see.''

She saw the heat in his eyes and immediately recalled the enticing feel of his touch. Suddenly his gaze turned cold, and she got the distinct feeling he would rather have been anywhere else but at her door. Well, she didn't want him there any more than he wanted to be there. Her life was complicated enough at the moment. "So now you don't have to give me another moment's thought."

Peter wished that were so. But he had a mission to complete. When she started to close the door, he placed his hand against it, stopping her. "Nice place," he said looking over her shoulder into the interior of her apartment.

That he seemed intent on remaining puzzled her. Reminding herself that he had saved her life and offered her shelter, she did what politeness demanded. "Would you like a cup of coffee?" she asked coolly.

"Sure, thanks."

As he entered, she was certain she saw a flash of uneasiness cross his features. Closing the door, she turned to face him. "Why are you here when you obviously don't want to be?" she demanded bluntly.

He scowled more at himself than at her. "I've developed this sort of big-brother attitude toward you. I guess it has something to do with saving your life. I'd hate to see you throw it away. Maybe Charles is a nice guy who made a mistake, or maybe he's a heel. I just figured someone should try to find out, before you made any decision about your future."

She could barely believe her ears. "And you, a person who would have been happy never to have met me, think you can make that determination?"

"I figure as an impersonal observer I can make a reasonable judgment."

She frowned at him. "I'd prefer to do this on my own."

And he should let her do just that, he told himself once again. Still he'd come a long way to soothe his conscience. "Since I'm here, I might as well stick around and meet Charles."

"Men," she muttered, heading into the kitchen. Getting down a mug, she watched him out of the corner of her eye. He stopped in the doorway. His open coat revealed a bulky sweater in place of his plaid shirt. To her chagrin, her gaze traveled lower to his muscular thighs and remained there. A heat curled through her. She didn't need lusty thoughts about Peter Whitley confusing her any more than she was already confused, she fumed. "You being here will just cause trouble," she said curtly.

"Can I assume by that remark that Charles saw us on television and jumped to the wrong conclusion?" Peter found himself feeling pleased to be the fly in the ointment. *Only because the guy deserves a little of what he dished out,* he assured himself.

"Yes," she replied, glad she could use Charles as the reason for getting rid of him. She didn't want him guessing she was still having erotic reactions to him. "I convinced him nothing happened. But if he finds you here, that could raise doubts and complicate an already-difficult situation."

"I'm certain I can convince him nothing happened." Getting those words out in a casual tone hadn't been easy. He'd been recalling the way her curves had molded to him, and the desire to see if she felt as good now as she had at his cabin was strong. *This is strictly a "hands off" situation,* he reminded himself.

Handing him the mug of coffee, Ellen's fingers brushed against his, and a current of power raced up her arm. Peter Whitley was a distraction she didn't need or want. "Why don't you just take care of whatever business brought you to town, and I'll take care of my business. Don't you need to hurry back to look after Bane, or did you bring him with you?"

"He's being looked after by Jack's neighbor." Peter could still feel the gentle brush of her fingertips against his skin, and the memories of their late-night encounter grew stronger. So maybe he wasn't being entirely honest about why he'd come to Boston. If her love for Charles was dead, he might consider pursuing her. But first he'd make certain she wasn't on the rebound.

"It appears that the sound is broken on your television," he observed, returning to the living room.

"I put it on mute while I was on the phone and never took it off," she replied, picking up the remote and turning off the set entirely.

Peter wasn't paying any attention. He was looking at the flowers. "Looks like a florist shop in here."

"They're from Charles." Wanting to keep a distance between them, she motioned for him to be seated in a chair, then seated herself on the couch as far from him as possible.

"An expensive apology," Peter noted.

"He can afford it. Not only is he a vice president at Tucker, his father owns the place." Seeing a sarcastic scowl spread over Peter's face, she added quickly, "But Charles is good at his job. He isn't just a figurehead. He knows the business."

Peter barely heard her. He was too busy calling himself a sucker. "I understand your problem now," he said. "It has to be hard to consider giving up a wealthy husband, even one you're not certain you can trust."

Realizing the scowl had been directed at her, not at Charles, her shoulders straightened. "His wealth has nothing to do with it!"

Peter raised a disbelieving eyebrow.

Anger toward his judgmental attitude bubbled to the surface. "I didn't ask for you to butt into my life. So just get out!" Rising, she headed to the door intending to fling it open for him.

"You're right. My nose doesn't belong in your business," he said, setting aside the mug and following. This was the last time he let a woman get under his skin, he vowed.

Her hand was on the knob when a knock sounded from the other side. *What now?* she wondered, as she opened it.

"Mr. Tucker decided to switch to live plants," the deliveryman said, picking up the potted palm beside him. "Where would you like me to put it?"

She could feel Peter's critical gaze. "Back in your store," she snapped.

The man looked disconcerted. "It's been paid for."

Feeling guilty for venting her anger on him, Ellen grimaced apologetically. "I'm sorry." She made a waving motion with her hand toward the interior of the apartment. "You can put it in the corner in the living room."

The man carried the palm inside, then hurried out, clearly afraid she might change her mind and make him take it with him.

"A potted palm?" Peter observed sarcastically.

Ellen glared at him. "Charles proposed to me beside a potted palm. It was New Year's Eve and he said he wanted to make this year the best year of his life. And to do that, all I had to do was to agree to marry him. But it's my guess you wouldn't understand romance if it hit you over the head."

"I hope I haven't come at a bad time?" a woman's voice interjected before Peter had a chance to respond.

Jerking around, Ellen came face-to-face with Charles's mother. Pretty, petite, always stylishly dressed and coiffured, with impeccable manners, Loretta Tucker was the epitome of elegance and decorum. Ellen doubted that the woman had ever raised her voice in anger, much less created a scene in public. A flush of embarrassment reddened her cheeks. "Mrs. Tucker...Loretta...I was just explaining why Charles had sent a potted palm," she managed to choke out.

But Loretta was paying no attention to her. Instead she was peering around Ellen at Peter. "I didn't realize your cousin was visiting." Passing Ellen, she extended her hand. "Mr. Whitley, isn't it? I'm Loretta Tucker."

Accepting the handshake, Peter considered setting the record straight. But if Ellen Reese wanted to build her world on lies, it wasn't up to him to expose her. Eventually they'd catch up with her.

"It must have been very rewarding to rescue that family," Loretta commented, breaking the sudden silence that had fallen over the trio.

"It was," he replied.

She turned to Ellen. "For both of you."

"Yes." There was a look on Loretta's face that reminded Ellen of her mother when her mother was about to impart advice or issue a warning. She guessed that after witnessing her tirade and having met Peter, the woman was questioning the "cousin" story, and Ellen prepared herself for a subtle, but sharp, accusation and declaration of war.

Unexpectedly, Loretta's expression returned to its usual polite calm and she glanced at her watch. "I really have to run. I know you and Charles have had a falling-out. He won't tell me what about, but he's absolutely devastated. He asked me to come by and plead for him. However, I feel you two should work this out on your own."

Ellen could detect no hint of what Loretta hoped would be the outcome. But then, she had noticed that where her husband and son were concerned, Loretta accepted their decisions without protest or comment. Ellen had, however, harbored the notion that behind closed doors Loretta made her feelings known. Now she wondered if even that was true. The woman seemed perfectly willing to allow Charles to follow whatever path he chose. "It was nice of you stop by," she said politely, unable to think of anything else.

Loretta smiled demurely then turned to Peter. "Perhaps we'll have a chance to meet again while you're in town. Are you staying here with Ellen?"

Her tone was casual, but the implication behind her question was not lost on him. He was certain she thought they'd had an affair and was asking if they planned to continue. His fair side demanded that he come to Ellen's defense. "No. As you've probably already surmised, we don't get along very well. I'm staying with an old professor of mine from the university."

Loretta studied him closely. "I've always found Ellen

very easy to get along with. In fact, that's one of the traits that my son loves so much.''

''Unlike Charles, my cousin can be self-righteous and judgmental,'' Ellen interjected sharply.

Peter shrugged. ''I simply call the shots as I see them.''

''Then I suggest you have your eyes examined.'' Suddenly remembering they weren't alone, she flushed and turned to Loretta. ''I'm sorry. As you can see, we have a hard time being civil to each other, that's why our paths so rarely cross. In fact,'' she added pointedly, ''if I have my way, they will never cross again.''

''There does appear to be a great deal of friction between the two of you,'' Loretta observed. A spark of amusement showed in her eyes. ''I'm a little surprised either of you survived the weekend in that cabin unscathed.''

Uncertain of what to say, Ellen was trying to think of something, when she noticed that Loretta's attention had again turned fully to Peter. ''I've taken several courses at the university,'' the woman said. ''Perhaps I know your professor.''

''Ian Cochran,'' Peter replied to the question in her voice.

''Oh, yes. Professor Cochran…archaeology. Fascinating subject.'' Again she extended her hand toward him. ''I'm sure Ellen didn't really mean what she said. Perhaps you can come to dinner one night.''

Ellen gave him a look that dared him to take Loretta up on the invitation. ''He won't be staying in town long.'' Recalling the lie she'd used earlier, she added, ''His father's ill. That was the reason I went up there.''

Feeling as if he'd been caught in the middle of a bad

farce, Peter forced an apologetic smile. "I don't want to be away from my ill father for too long. I'm just here to do some quick research and consult with Ian. Because of a sense of duty, I stopped by to see Ellen. But she's right, it would be best if our paths don't cross too often."

"Well, I'm glad I got to meet you." Loretta gave him a smile, then with a nod and smile in Ellen's direction, she left, pulling the door closed behind her.

"Cousin? Sick father?" Peter said caustically as soon as they were alone.

Ellen faced him defiantly. "I added the sick father to explain what kind of family business had called me away so urgently. But the cousin bit wasn't my doing. Right after the broadcast, before I'd even had a chance to tell Charles that nothing had happened between us, he told everyone you were my cousin. He said he blamed himself for anything rash I'd done and wanted to protect me from gossip." Her shoulders stiffened even more. "And I'm grateful to him for that. Do you have any idea how embarrassing it would have been for me to show up at work and have people whispering about me behind my back?"

Peter regarded her dryly. "Obviously the man's a paragon as well as being wealthy."

"Yes, he is," she retorted.

"However, I'm not too sure the mother bought the 'cousin' routine. And don't you think the sick father was a little on the melodramatic side?"

"It seemed like the only reasonable explanation as to why I'd set foot under your roof."

"Lies always catch up with people," he cautioned acidly.

"You're probably right," she conceded, already regretting having mentioned the sick father to Loretta. She had not minded playing along with Charles to save them both embarrassment. But she was not used to lying, and adding her own embellishments was beginning to cause a bitter taste in her mouth. Opening the door, she said, "Please leave."

"Gladly." Telling himself he would be happy if he never saw Ellen Reese again, Peter strode out.

Relieved to finally be alone, Ellen drew a harsh breath. Even if Loretta hadn't bought the "cousin" routine, Peter had made it clear there was nothing between them. She told herself that she should be grateful, but she hated feeling beholden to such an arrogant, self-righteous boor.

"Good riddance!" she muttered under her breath.

Peter sat glowering into the fire he'd built upon returning to Ian's home. He'd been a fool to think Ellen Reese might need someone to look after her.

"I'd hate to be the object of that anger on your face," Ian said, easing himself into his favorite chair. "Can I assume you met Charles and don't approve of him?"

Peter had been so intent on his own thoughts, he hadn't heard his host arriving home. "No. I haven't met Charles. But I have seen the real Miss Reese, and I wish Charles the best of luck. He'll be needing it."

"That sounds rather ominous," Ian noted.

"She's a liar and a gold digger. I can't believe I let myself get fooled by a woman again."

"A liar and a gold digger? Those are pretty harsh accusations."

"I can understand the lie," Peter admitted grudgingly. "And if it happened the way she said it did, then I might be being a little unfair on that point. But she is a gold digger. Her fiancé is Charles Tucker of Tucker, Inc. She's just playing him along, making him squirm to get her hooks deeper into him. Then she'll reel him in, hook, line and sinker."

Ian studied him thoughtfully. "I thought you were worried about the fiancé being the heel. Didn't you tell me he had an affair with another woman?"

"Too bad for him, but lucky for Miss Reese. She should be able to use that indiscretion to her advantage for the entire length of their marriage. It's my guess she'll never let him live it down."

Ian frowned. "Are you sure you aren't having a knee-jerk reaction...putting too much of your former wife into this Ellen Reese? You were young and naive about women when you married Nancy. And, as I've always suspected, you never really worked through your anger when she betrayed you."

Peter hunched further down in his chair. "Ellen caught her fiancé with another woman. It hurt her so badly she got herself into a life-and-death situation. I'll bet if he wasn't wealthy, she'd never consider taking him back."

"Or it could be that she really loves the man...or *did* love him, and now that love has been damaged and she's uncertain about what to do. Some women do have honest feelings. My Rachel did."

Peter continued to glower at the fire. "You're right about Nancy. I was furious with her for betraying me, but I was angrier with myself. I'd bought into all her lies. I felt like a fool. You warned me about her, but I wouldn't listen."

"She was a real looker." Ian eyed him speculatively. "Miss Reese appeared to be a little more down-to-earth in the looks department. Of course, the reception on my television wasn't very good."

"She's nice enough looking. Nothing spectacular. Brownest eyes I've ever seen. Nice curves." Suddenly realizing his voice had become husky, Peter clamped his mouth shut.

Ian's grinned. "So you were attracted to her?"

"I've been without female companionship for a while."

"And did she show any signs of being attracted to you?" Ian probed.

"Whatever attraction there was between us was purely physical." Seeing the glimmer in the old man's eyes, Peter realized Ian thought he'd taken Ellen to bed. He felt it was only fair to set the record straight. "But I didn't let it go far. At the time I figured she was either having a rebound reaction or wanted to hurt Charles by giving herself to a stranger."

"In which case, she would have had to be in love with the man," Ian surmised.

"Or maybe she just got tired of practicing abstinence and decided to have a little fun."

Ian raised an eyebrow. "Abstinence?"

"She claimed she was...is a virgin."

"You seemed to have found out quite a lot about the woman," Ian noted.

"More than enough," Peter growled.

"If she is a virgin, then your 'gold digger' theory doesn't work," Ian persisted. "If Charles thought he was getting unused goods, then giving in to you could put her future with him at risk."

Peter shrugged. "Once the vows were exchanged what difference would her virginity or nonvirginity make? Besides, if he noticed, I'm sure she could come up with a convincing lie."

"So now what do you do about Miss Reese?"

Peter's jaw firmed. "Nothing. She goes her way, and I go mine."

"You aren't considering informing the fiancé of your suspicions, are you? There is the possibility you might be misjudging Miss Reese."

"No, I'm not going to interfere. Besides, the man's in love. I figure he wouldn't listen, anyway."

Ian nodded his approval.

Peter drew a terse breath. "She even fooled Bane. He accepted her presence easily. After she left, he actually acted as if he missed her."

"I've always been under the impression that wolf was a good judge of character."

"Women can boggle any male mind," Peter grumbled. Then straightening, he rose from the chair. "Let's go get some dinner. I'm buying. We'll talk archaeology and geology and forget about Miss Reese."

Chapter Seven

Ellen sat waiting. In addition to reminders of the good times they'd had, each note accompanying the flowers and plant sent by Charles had pleaded with her to have dinner with him. She glanced at the clock. He should be arriving anytime now, unless he'd spoken to his mother, found out that Peter was in town, jumped to the conclusion she'd lied to him and decided she was not worth pursuing.

That possibility should upset her, she thought. And maybe in a week or even tomorrow it would. Right now, all she felt was numb. The scent of the roses permeated the air. Was she overreacting...letting one indiscretion destroy what could be a lifetime of happiness?

She looked down at her jeans and sweatshirt. An hour ago she'd considered changing and decided against it. It had been a long day, and she was in no mood to go out in public. Besides, she couldn't be certain Charles would even show up.

Peter wandered into her thoughts, and she frowned. If he'd been her fiancé instead of Charles and he'd been unfaithful, she'd have had no trouble making the decision to kick him out of her life. His flowers and potted palm would have been out on the sidewalk waiting for the trash pickup. The man was an irritant. She'd never met anyone who could make her so angry with just a mere glance.

Of course he did have his good qualities, her fair side insisted on pointing out. He'd gone out into a blizzard to rescue her and she'd seen the compassion on his face for the Pyresses when they'd found the downed plane.

She also recalled his declaration that he would never betray a woman he loved. She didn't know what made her so certain he would keep his word, but she was. "Because he probably couldn't find anyone else to bed," she muttered, refusing to think too many good thoughts about him. After all, he'd made it clear he thought she was after Charles's money. But the memory of how erotic his touch could be returned to dispute this caustic conclusion. Groaning, she slouched further into her chair. Why was she even thinking of that bearded boor? She shoved him out of her mind and again concentrated on Charles.

Would he come or would he not? She plucked a daisy from the bouquet that had arrived half an hour earlier, reminding her of a picnic they'd gone on last summer, and began pulling out the petals. As she worked her way around the perimeter, the question changed to did she care or did she not?

A knock sounded on her door. Well, someone had arrived.

It was Charles.

"You look terrible," he said with concern, placing a hand on her forehead as he entered and closed the door. "Are you ill?"

"I'm just tired and confused." There had been a time when his touch was comforting, now it irritated her. She backed out of his reach.

Angry accusation replaced his concern. "My mother told me your 'cousin' was here today. I'd guess from your drained appearance you were not totally honest with me about what happened in that cabin."

Defiance flashed in her eyes. "Nothing happened! Peter Whitley came into town to do some research and talk to a former professor...Ian Cochran, I think he said. He stopped by here to see if I had gotten back all right."

"He could have simply called."

"And I wish he had." Again recalling the accusations Peter had tossed at her caused a fresh burst of fury. "Actually, I wish he'd never left New Hampshire. I don't think I've ever met a man who is so absolutely disagreeable."

Charles's expression relaxed, and he placed an arm around her shoulders. "He gave you a rough time?"

She told herself to make some noncommittal remark and let the subject drop. Instead, she heard herself saying, "The truth is, he sees himself as a Boy Scout, protecting the innocent. I'd told him about you and Janet. After I left, he appointed himself my big brother. He came to town to make certain you weren't a heel, and that if I did marry you, you would treat me right." She met Charles's gaze. "But when he found out you were wealthy, he accused me of wanting to marry you for your money. He said it was your wealth that was causing me to be so indecisive about forgiving you. But that's not true."

Charles smiled reassuringly. "Of course it's not true. I don't know of any other woman who is more forthright and honest than you."

A nudging of guilt assailed her. "I did tell one small lie today."

He raised a questioning eyebrow.

"I told Marilyn I'd gone to New Hampshire because Mr. Whitley's father was gravely ill and wanted to see me. And I told your mother that his father was ill, also. At the time it seemed like an easy solution. Marilyn knew I'd told Paul I needed time off for a family emergency, and I wanted your mother to think Peter would be leaving town very soon so she wouldn't invite him to dinner." She breathed a tired sigh. "I didn't enjoy lying though. Especially to your mother."

"You chose a perfect solution. And you shouldn't consider it lying. You should consider it damage control."

"I suppose," she conceded.

Charles drew her into his embrace. "As soon as you forgive me, we can both put all of this out of our minds."

Ellen recalled how safe, secure and cozy she'd felt in his arms in the past. She leaned her cheek against his shoulder and tried hard to recapture that feeling. It wouldn't come. "It's been a long day, and I'm not going to be good company." Gently but firmly, she attempted to free herself.

Sighing, Charles released her. Then lifting her chin with the tips of his fingers, he forced her to meet his gaze. "I was willing to forgive you. I'm begging you to forgive me. It was you I wanted to be with."

She wanted to believe him, but in her mind's eye she recalled the smile on his face when he'd opened the door Saturday night. It reminded her of the cat who'd caught the canary. Or maybe shock was affecting her memory and making her see it that way. "I want a husband I can trust."

"You can trust me. I swear I've learned my lesson."

Frustration swept through her. Stepping away from his touch, she raked her fingers through her hair and tried hard to accept him at his word. "I suppose I am being naive. These are modern times. I should be more open-minded."

Circling behind her, he placed his hands on her shoulders and guided her to her favorite chair. "For now, just let me take care of you. You sit and relax. I'm going out for Chinese. We'll eat, then you can go to bed and get a good night's sleep. Tomorrow I'll again pursue you diligently. I love you, Ellen, and I intend to marry you."

She leaned back in the chair and shut her eyes as the door closed behind him. He was so sincere. Why couldn't she do as he asked and put this whole sordid business behind them? *Because I'm too pedestrian, too Victorian, too closed minded?* she accused. Her jaw firmed. "No. Because I want a husband I don't have suspicions about when he says he's working late at the office!"

Pushing herself out of the chair, she rose and began moving from one bouquet to the other. As more had arrived during the remainder of the afternoon, she'd been forced to spread them around the apartment. Reading each note, her mind replayed Charles's courtship. He'd been romantic and charming. He'd made her laugh, and she'd easily envisioned the two of them posing for a family portrait with two small children and a third on the way.

That portrait would certainly be different from any Peter Whitley might pose in, she mused. The image of her and him with two small children...the children dressed in buckskins, him in his plaid shirt and jeans, and her, pregnant, wearing a loose-fitting calico dress...played through her mind, and she sneered. Then a corner of her mouth quirked upward and the sneer vanished. The kids looked cute, and Peter didn't look as out of place as she'd thought he would.

She rubbed her face hard, erasing the picture from her mind. "Why does that man keeping popping into my mind?" she growled. "And with kids, no less!"

A knock announced Charles's return. Grateful for any diversion from the paths her thoughts were traveling, she hurried to let him in.

She'd been certain she wouldn't be able to eat, but as he unpacked the food her stomach growled, reminding her how little she'd eaten during the day. To her relief he kept his word about not pressuring her and allowed her to eat in relative silence. After which, she pleaded exhaustion and asked him to leave.

"Say you'll join me for lunch in my office tomorrow," he pleaded.

She told herself that she should give their relationship every chance to return to the way it had been. "I'll be back at work tomorrow. As long as nothing goes wrong and they don't need me on the line, I'll be there."

He smiled warmly. "Good." Then drawing her into his arms, he kissed her.

She didn't fight him.

Lifting his head away, his smile became even warmer. "Can I assume that you're beginning to forgive me?"

"I wanted to see how kissing you would feel," she replied honestly.

"And?"

She'd found herself thinking about him kissing Janet, and the urge to brush the feel of his lips away with the back of her hand was strong. But she chose not to do that or inform him of her thoughts. Instead she simply said, "It's not the same as it was before."

Purpose showed on his face. "It will be."

"I'd like for it to be," she admitted.

"That's a good start." He winked, dropped a kiss on the tip of her nose, and left.

Returning to the kitchen to tidy up, she found herself wondering what Charles would look like in a beard. In the next instant the feel of Peter's beard against her neck returned to taunt her. Furious that she'd again let him into her thoughts, she tossed the rest of the cartons into the trash and went in to take a shower.

"You have a visitor," Ian announced.

Peter had risen to place another log on the fire while Ian had gone to answer the door. Both had been surprised that anyone would come by so late. Straightening, he saw a handsome, blond-haired man, about his height, striding toward him. Cold anger was etched into the caller's features.

"I'm Charles Tucker," the newcomer introduced himself curtly.

Good looks and wealthy, Peter thought dryly. Miss Reese had found herself a catch. "Mr. Tucker." He extended his hand toward the man.

Refusing the handshake, Charles came to a halt and glowered at Peter. "I want you to leave Ellen alone. She and I will work out our differences on our own. We don't need any interference from the likes of you. If it had not been for my quick thinking, her reputation would have been ruined."

Peter told himself he should feel sorry for the man. Instead he found Charles's pompous, authoritarian manner grating. "If it hadn't been for you, she would never have placed her life or her reputation in danger."

A sneer tilted one corner of Charles's mouth. "Her naiveté and innocence make her a very appealing woman. I suppose you came here hoping to catch her on the rebound."

Peter had been considering subtle ways to warn the man that he was heading for trouble. Now he lost interest in breaking the news to him gently. "Has it ever occurred to you that she's only interested in you because of your money?"

Charles laughed. "You obviously don't know her well at all. Ellen can't be bought. That's one of the reasons I find her so intriguing. In addition, she's intelligent...too intelligent for a backwoods barbarian like you. She's also loyal and honest. Two qualities I cherish deeply in a woman. And I intend to marry her. So stay away."

Peter watched in silence as the man brushed past Ian, slamming the door closed behind him as he exited.

"What was that business about his quick thinking saving Miss Reese's reputation?" Ian asked when the vibrations from the slamming of the door ceased.

"He told everyone I was her cousin."

Ian nodded. "That was quick thinking."

"She's obviously got him wrapped around her little finger," Peter muttered.

"Well, if she has, he deserves it." Ian seated himself once again. "I don't like people who think they're better than others, and I got the distinct feeling that's exactly what he thinks...barging in here, calling you a backwoods barbarian." Ian suddenly laughed. "Although, you do look like one."

Peter, too, returned to his chair. "I wasn't impressed by him, either. But I still don't like to see a man made a fool of."

Ian studied him sharply. "Are we talking about you or Mr. Tucker?"

Peter made no comment.

"If you're wrong about Miss Reese, then I feel sorry for her," Ian said. "Did you notice he never used the word *love* in describing his feelings for her. He said she was 'intriguing' because she couldn't be bought. That sounds as if he saw her as a challenge. Then there was the mention of her naiveté and innocence making her appealing. And that business about her being 'loyal and honest'...for some reason I couldn't help thinking he was describing a pet rather than a wife."

"Ellen Reese can take care of herself." But even as he made this declaration, Peter was having his doubts. He recalled how hurt she'd looked when he'd first found her. And the anger and frustration she'd expressed toward Charles had seemed genuine. Leaning back in his chair, he drew a tired breath. "Maybe I am letting old memories affect me too much." The frown on his face deepened. "Or maybe not. Why would any woman put up with that pompous ass if it wasn't for his money?"

"Maybe he hides that side of his character from her," Ian suggested. "Men can be as devious as women, when it comes to getting what they want."

"I suppose that's possible. I was going to stick around for a while, anyway. I really do need to do some research and go over a few theories with you."

Ian grinned. "Stay as long as you like."

Loretta Tucker stood at the window in her parlor, sipping wine and watching her son coming up the front steps. He reminded her of a man in control of his world. She lifted her glass in a silent salute. He and his father were very much alike. The potted palm had been a nice touch.

"Mother?" Charles said, pausing at her door to look in. "I thought you had a charity function to attend tonight."

"Your father had to work late, and I didn't feel like going alone." She forced a smile. "Can I assume that things went well with Ellen tonight?"

"She's still upset with me." He sighed impatiently. "You women take these lovers' quarrels much too seriously."

"You never said what you quarreled about."

He regarded her indulgently. "It was nothing important. Silly, actually."

"Did Mr. Whitley have anything to do with it?" she asked bluntly.

"No. He's merely a nuisance, and I took care of him tonight. He will not be interfering any further."

Loretta frowned thoughtfully. "He didn't seem like a man who could easily be brushed aside."

"He's a Neanderthal. A dolt. In other words, someone we have no need to give a second thought to."

Loretta took another sip of her wine to bolster her courage. "I know you don't appreciate my interfering in your life, but are you so very certain Ellen will fit into our little family?"

He scowled darkly. "She will fit in just fine. Perhaps it was just as well Mr. Whitley was there this afternoon and you didn't get a chance to talk to her." His gaze narrowed accusingly on her. "You're in one of your moods and drinking again." He sighed agitatedly. "Am I going to have to make reservations at the clinic for you?"

She scowled back. "I'm in one of my moods, but I'm not drunk nor do I intend to be. This is my one and only glass for the evening."

"I think it would be best if you stayed away from Ellen for now." It was an order, not a request.

Loretta raised her glass in a gesture of acquiescence.

Crossing the room, he kissed her on the forehead. "Good night, mother."

"Good night, son," she said to his departing back.

As his footsteps retreated down the hall, she set her glass aside. She would drink no more tonight. She wanted a clear head for tomorrow.

Ellen, dressed in a plain cotton nightgown, wandered around her apartment again going from bouquet to bouquet. Was there some truth in Peter Whitley's accusation? Was she letting the trappings of wealth influence her? Was that why she was still considering marrying Charles?

She didn't like to think she could be bought. Yes, she'd enjoyed the places he took her and the parties. But that wasn't why she'd agreed to marry him. It was his gentleness and his sincerity. Granted, she was aware that those who knew him through business deals didn't think of him that way. He could be tough. He'd been tough on her during their first meeting. But he'd made up for that. He'd proved to have the soul of a romantic. The flowers and the potted palm were evidence of that.

And when he'd thought she'd been intimate with Peter Whitley, he'd been willing to forgive her, even place the blame on his own shoulders. He was a forgiving, gentle, sincere man. So he'd made one mistake. They weren't married yet. As even the judgmental Mr. Whitley had pointed out, a lot of men have one last fling. She should be ecstatic to have Charles be in love with her. He'd even removed Janet from their lives so she would not be a constant reminder and embarrassment.

"Then why don't I feel pleased?" she demanded. "Because I'm too tired to think straight," she answered, and, turning off the lights, went to bed.

Chapter Eight

Loretta Tucker knocked on the door of Professor Ian Cochran's town house. It was mid-morning. "Catching the bear in his lair," she murmured under her breath. A faint smile tilted the corners of her mouth.

Alone inside, Peter answered the door. "Mrs. Tucker," he said, making no effort to hide his surprise.

Her smile deepened. "Mr. Whitley."

He read the purpose in her eyes and immediately his guard came up. "To what do I owe this visit?"

"It's rather brisk out here. You could ask me in," she suggested.

Stepping aside, he allowed her to pass him.

"And where may we sit and talk?" she asked, pausing a couple of steps beyond the door.

"There's a fire in the living room," he replied, motioning toward an open door. Her confident air and continued smile was making him uneasy. He'd never liked cat-and-mouse games, especially when he had the feeling he was to be the mouse.

Entering the room he'd indicated, she seated herself. Peter followed, but remained standing.

"I'm not certain what transpired between you and my son last night. I can only assume that you upset Ellen, and Charles told you to stay away from her." She unbuttoned her coat and eased herself more comfortably into her chair as she spoke. "I realize that personality clashes among family members is a common occurrence. But, family is family. I've always felt strongly that an effort should be made to keep peace and harmony within the ranks."

"I don't think peace and harmony will ever describe mine and Ellen's relationship."

"And yet she ran to you when she and my son had a quarrel." Clearly expecting him to deny this, she held up a hand like a policeman stopping traffic. "And don't try to tell me that it was concern for a sick uncle that took her there. That's much too convenient an excuse. Charles did something to upset her, and she took off and landed on your doorstep."

Peter was more convinced than ever that the woman didn't believe he was Ellen's cousin. He was also certain Loretta Tucker was searching for a weapon to use against Miss Reese. And, although he was still not convinced Ellen Reese was not a gold digger, he didn't like the idea of being used as a pawn in whatever game Mrs. Tucker was planning.

However, he didn't relish lying, either. But a few inferences in the wrong direction weren't exactly a lie. "Actually she wasn't expecting to find me. The cabin belongs to a longtime family friend. Currently he's in Arizona. Ellen wasn't aware of that, and she wasn't aware that I was staying at the cabin."

"I see." Loretta glanced around the room. "I was hoping to meet your wolf. He looked like a magnificent creature."

"Bane is not *my* wolf. He adopted Jack and considers the cabin his home. He never leaves those woods."

For a long moment Loretta studied him speculatively, then asked, "What do you do for a living, Mr. Whitley? May I call you Peter? After all, I know my son. Once he sets his mind to something he gets it. That means we will be family soon."

This thought brought a twinge of displeasure. If Ellen Reese was the person he'd first thought she was and the woman Charles had described, she deserved better than an overbearing husband and an interfering mother-in-law. On the other hand, she could know exactly what she was getting into and be willing to put up with it for the lifestyle Charles could provide. "I have a consulting business."

"And just what do you consult about?"

In spite of the woman's friendly manner, Peter was well aware that he was being interrogated. "I study rock and soil formations and tell the landowners if there is a possibility they might find something of value beyond what the eye can see. Then, if they are willing to pay my price, I make an attempt to find it."

"Something of value?" she prodded.

"Gold. Gemstones. Silver. Copper, et cetera."

Understanding flashed in her eyes. "You're a prospector."

"I suppose that's as good a description as any."

"And you actually make a living at it?" A musing frown caused her mouth to form a thoughtful pout. "Or do you simply move from friend's house to friend's house between jobs?''

The insinuation that he might be a freeloader raised his ire. "I make a respectable living. If you're worried about my showing up on your son's doorstep after he and Ellen are married, I can assure that will never happen.''

She frowned as if displeased with herself. "No, of course it won't. I apologize, Mr. Whitley. It was crass of me to ask about your financial situation." Smiling politely, she rose and buttoned her coat. "I appreciate your seeing me," she said, heading to the door. As he opened it for her, she paused before completing her exit. "Perhaps you and Ellen will mend your differences and I will see you at the wedding.''

"Perhaps." *But only if hell freezes over,* he added silently, watching her descend the steps.

Loretta climbed into her car and pulled away. At the first red light she looked up a number in her address book and punched it into her cellular phone.

A woman answered.

"I have a very discreet job for you.''

"Discretion is my forte.''

"I want a complete bio on a Peter Whitley...financial status, lifestyle, family connections, et cetera. And I need it right away. He's staying with Professor Ian Cochran at the moment." She gave the professor's address. "No one must know about this.''

"I'll handle this one myself," the woman on the other end promised.

Peter was disliking the Tuckers more and more.

Slowly, attempting to recall every detail, he recounted his association with Ellen Reese. He'd thought she was genuine up until he'd learned of Charles's wealth. Had he become too cynical? Was he letting past experience affect his judgment?

His mind traveled back ten years, and for the first time, he took a long, cold look at himself and Nancy. The signs of her greed had always been there. He'd just refused to recognize them. He'd been young and in love. "Live and learn," he muttered to himself.

But had he learned his lesson or could a pleasant face and soft body still warp his reason? His jaw tensed. He wasn't ready to trust Ellen Reese. However, he also couldn't bring himself to desert her to the Tuckers. Not just yet, anyway.

Ellen sat at her workbench. She had two pumps in pieces in front of her. She was supposed to be determining which would be the best to replace an old model that was constantly breaking down. Instead she'd spent the morning absentmindedly disassembling each pump while trying to determine her real feelings toward Charles.

She glanced down at her ring finger and said a silent thank-you to whoever wrote the plant safety regulations. They forbade the wearing of jewelry in the working areas. Afraid that if she left her ring locked in her desk all day, she'd forget it, she'd quickly fallen into the habit of leaving it at home. So the fact that she wasn't wearing it had not raised any eyebrows or prompted any questions from her fellow workers.

"Time for lunch," Paul Saunders's voice broke into her thoughts. "And Charles asked me to tell you to bring your coat."

Startled, she jerked around to see her supervisor at the door of her lab. "Is it that late already?"

"It's a quarter to twelve." He shifted a little uneasily. "Charles made it clear to me that my job was on the line if I didn't see that you got to his office on time."

A sense of déjà vu swept through her. Suddenly she was recalling an incident a few months earlier when Paul had come looking for her out in the plant and said the same thing to her. She'd protested that she needed to finish what she was doing but he'd ordered her to leave, saying Charles's orders had been specific and it wasn't smart to disobey the guy at the top. She'd been flattered that Charles had been so insistent on her company. This time, however, she took a close look at Paul. He was smiling that forced smile she'd labeled his "attempting to hide his worry" smile. An unpleasant thought occurred to her. "You don't really think he'd fire you just because I didn't make it to lunch on time, do you?"

He shrugged. "I'd rather not take the chance. I've got a wife and three kids to feed."

She'd heard grumblings about Charles using his position to bully people, but she'd thought they were merely the complaints of people he'd had to call on the carpet for not doing their jobs properly. "I wouldn't want to do anything to jeopardize you or them."

Concern replaced Paul's weak smile. "Look I didn't mean to imply that I don't think your fiancé is a fair man. He's the boss. He's used to getting his way."

She'd been too caught up in falling in love to take a close look at what was happening around her. Now she realized that Paul had been treating her differently these past weeks. He didn't question her ideas, and he rarely came by just to chat like he had when she'd first come to work here. Also there was her call to him last Saturday night when she'd asked to take a few vacation days. He hadn't balked at all. Now she read the worry in his eyes and knew he was afraid she might make some crack to Charles that would cost him his job. She smiled reassuringly. "I'll be certain to tell him that you're taking good care of me and made certain I didn't skip my lunch hour."

"Yeah, thanks," he replied and left.

After quickly washing her hands and changing out of the protective jumpsuit she'd been wearing, and back into her slacks and sweater, she grabbed her coat and strode toward Charles's office. Maybe she'd misjudged Paul's reaction. Maybe what she'd thought were fears about Charles were actually overreactions because of a fight Paul had had with his wife that morning. Or maybe Paul was more insecure than she'd thought. Maybe it was his nature to worry unnecessarily.

Harriet Masters, Charles's secretary, smiled up at her as she entered Charles's outer office. "He's waiting for you."

Ellen smiled back at the motherly looking, middle-aged widow. Out of the corner of her eye, she noticed the flower on Harriet's desk. Every week there was a fresh rose in the vase, compliments of Charles. Harriet had once described it as one of the lovely little perks she got for working for such a wonderful employer. Ellen was well aware that the woman was as loyal to Charles as a lapdog. No one, who did not want to be summarily berated and have their words repeated to Charles, would ever say anything derogatory about him in front of her.

A true bully wouldn't inspire that kind of devotion, she reasoned as she continued into his office.

"You look lovely," he said, rising from his desk and coming around to greet her. Reaching her, he took out his handkerchief. "No other woman could ever wear a grease stain as well as you."

In the past she would have laughed lightly and, as he removed the smear with his handkerchief, would have experienced a warm, excited curl working its way through her. Today Janet's image popped into her mind, and she jerked away from him. "I suppose Janet wore…" She paused. Janet's work had involved a computer and telephone. However, she had taken messages. "…ink stains well."

Charles nodded approvingly. "That's good. Let all the anger out. I deserve it."

"I've never asked you about anything you did before we became engaged. I figured that was water under the bridge," she continued curtly, the thoughts she'd been holding captive until now pouring forth. "But after we became engaged, I expected fidelity."

"And you had a right to." Remorse showed in his features. "I was weak. I gave in to lust. But, I promise you, it will never happen again. When you left town and I couldn't find you, I thought I'd go mad."

He looked so miserable, she felt guilty. "I had to get away."

"I understand." He stroked her cheek. "But you have no idea how scared I was."

"I'm sorry."

He kissed her lightly on the nose. "I forgive you."

Realizing what had just happened, she stiffened. "I'm not the one who should be apologizing!"

"Come on. Admit it," he coaxed gently. "We were both wrong. I was more wrong than you. But if you had thrown yourself into Whitley's arms, I would have forgiven you. I'd even have taken the blame." He leered playfully. "You are so incredibly delicious looking when you're angry." When she continued to scowl, his expression once again became remorseful. "Please, don't throw away the life we planned because I behaved like a heel."

"I want a husband I can trust," she repeated.

He caressingly traced the line of her jaw. "You can trust me. At least give me a chance. I know you have a fair mind and a warm heart. You must understand that no one, not even me, is perfect."

"I never—" She paused in mid-sentence. She'd been about to declare that she'd never thought of him as being perfect, but that would have been a lie. She had. And he *had* been in her eyes...too perfect, she realized now. "Well, maybe I did see you that way," she conceded.

He smiled softly. "I'll settle for that as a breakthrough. Now, how about lunch?"

She nodded in agreement. "I suppose I wasn't being totally realistic," she said as he helped her with her coat.

He kissed her neck. "I was the one who behaved foolishly."

His lips were warm but the excitement was missing. She recalled the fire Peter had brought to life with a kiss on that spot. Charles had ignited that same kind of fire in the past, she reminded herself. Well, maybe it had been something more akin to heated embers, she corrected. But the comparison wasn't fair. That night in the cabin had been something not truly real. She'd been under stress. Her nerves had been taut and more sensitive to stimuli. Anything she'd felt those two days in the mountains was questionable and most certainly superficial. Peter Whitley had proved to be judgmental and arrogant. He could never inspire any real depth of feeling within her.

"Come along," Charles said, and she obeyed.

As they neared their exit, she heard a familiar whirling sound. Now she guessed why there had been a cordoned-off area in the parking lot when she'd arrived at work this morning. Stepping outside, she saw the helicopter.

"It's such a beautiful day, I thought lunch at a ski lodge overlooking the mountains would be nice," Charles explained, guiding her toward the chopper.

Climbing in, she told herself that she should be flattered that he would go to so much trouble to impress her. Instead she recalled hearing Stella Dorwood complaining about having to park so far from the building because of so many of the nearer spots being cordoned off. Ellen couldn't blame her. The wind had been bitter that morning and Stella was seven months pregnant. Now she wondered if Stella was watching from a window and mentally stewing over the inconvenience caused her by Charles's whim. The thought brought an uncomfortable pang of embarrassment.

"And after lunch we'll take a few runs down the slope," Charles yelled in her ear as they buckled themselves in.

"I don't have the right clothes for skiing," she reminded him.

He nodded toward two satchels. "The paisley one is

yours. I had Martha do a little shopping for you this morning.''

In the past she would have been flattered and awed by his generosity. Today, Peter Whitley's dour countenance calling her a "gold digger" popped into her mind.

"I'm not the boss. I can't just take the afternoon off.''

"But I am the boss, and I've already told Paul not to expect you back today.''

She knew from the determined set of Charles's jaw that arguing would be futile. She also knew that if she was any other employee, tomorrow Paul would call her in and reprimand her for taking half a day off on the spur of the moment for no reason other than to enjoy herself. But because she was being courted by Charles, he wouldn't say anything. He'd keep his feelings to himself, and that would lead to more strain between them. "I'll go along with you today. But we can't do this again. It's not fair for me to dump my workload on others.'' Silently she promised herself she'd speak to Paul, apologize for leaving for the afternoon and assure him she would not make a habit of it.

"You should learn to relax and enjoy the perks of being engaged to the boss,'' Charles admonished her.

She was going to remind him that as far as she was concerned, at the moment, they were no longer engaged, but the sound of the blades would have caused her to have to shout this information, and that didn't seem like the polite thing to do. Adding stress to her already strained nerves, Peter's cynical countenance continued to haunt her. *Well this wasn't her doing,* she snapped at it. This was all Charles's idea. Pushing the judgmental image from her mind, she sat back and watched the scenery as the machine lifted off the ground.

"How do you like the view?" Charles asked once they were in the air.

"Nice," she replied, hiding a rush of fear. She'd never told Charles, but she didn't like to fly. Although she'd flown without protest when it had been necessary, she'd never enjoyed it. In fact the only time she'd ever been comfortable in the air had been during the rescue of the Pyress family. Startled by this realization, she reasoned that she'd been so concerned about the children she hadn't had time to be afraid. Then she was forced to admit that even on the trip back to the crash site, she hadn't been nervous or worried. The thought that this sense of security had been because Peter had been with her played through her mind. Refusing to admit that the man could have been the reason she'd felt safe, she shoved the thought out. *I was simply too concerned about the Pyresses to worry about my own safety,* she told herself.

Charles had begun pointing out landmarks.

To her relief, because it required yelling to respond, he was satisfied with a smile and a nod.

By the time they landed, she'd been holding so tightly to the edge of her seat for so long, her hands almost refused to open. But they did, and she was able to alight with dignity.

During the ride in the ski lift to the restaurant at the summit, she tried to relax and recapture the sense of enjoyment she used to feel in Charles's company. Instead, she remained uneasy.

"I'm going to assume," he said, after they were seated at a window table and their drinks ordered, "that you're going to forgive me. I don't want to face the other possibility.'' He leaned closer to her and smiled beseechingly. ''So where do you want to go for a honeymoon? I was thinking of Paris or Venice. Both are beautiful in the spring.''

''I've never been to either one.'' She pictured herself and Charles strolling down a street in Paris then riding in a gondola in Venice. Instead of a rush of pleasure and excitement, the images only made her more tense. ''I don't think I'm ready to discuss honeymoon plans.''

Charles frowned. ''I never thought you could be so closed minded. Really, you're being very childish about this. I've groveled. What more do you want?''

''I never asked you to grovel,'' she returned tersely.

He regarded her pleadingly. ''What can I do to make things right?''

She shrugged. ''I don't know.'' The remorse in his eyes was making her feel as if she was being unreasonable. ''Maybe I am being childish. I've just never been very 'worldly.' ''

He smiled and again stroked her cheek. ''That is one of the qualities I love so much about you. And I hate myself for having betrayed so innocent a trust as yours.''

She looked into the blue depths of his eyes. They seemed shallow and pale. Realizing she was comparing them to Peter's, she swung her gaze to the slope.

''I'm trying too hard, aren't I?'' Charles captured her chin and forced her face gently back in his direction. ''How about if we don't talk about us? How about if we simply enjoy the food and the beauty of the day?''

What she wanted was to be alone, but avoiding Charles hadn't helped her make a decision about what she was going to do. Hopefully, spending the afternoon with him would. She forced a smile. "I'd like that."

Chapter Nine

But spending the afternoon with Charles hadn't solved anything, she admitted hours later as she sat alone in her apartment. He'd wanted to take her out to dinner, but she'd refused, pleading exhaustion. That hadn't been a lie. After lunch they'd skied. The exercise, combined with the struggle to hide her terror during the trips in the helicopter, had left her drained.

Charles had called twice since she'd gotten home. The first time to make certain she'd arrived safely and the second to ascertain that the gourmet dinner he'd ordered for her had arrived. Both times she thanked him for his concern and felt like a heel for not being able to forgive him.

Now, dressed in a pair of old sweatpants and a much-worn sweatshirt she sat on the couch eating the cheesecake that had come with the dinner. In front of her on the coffee table was the engagement ring he'd given her, its five-carat diamond sparkling in the lamplight.

Could she be blowing the best opportunity she would ever have? Charles could provide her with a life most women would envy. Even more, if she didn't marry him, she might never find anyone else. She could end up alone...no husband, no children.

A knock on the door brought a groan. She wasn't in the mood for company.

The knock sounded again.

Answering it, she stared at her caller. If it hadn't been for those distinctive blue eyes, she wasn't certain she would have recognized him. His hair had been cut, and his beard and mustache were gone.

"Guess I look a little different," Peter said, rubbing his clean-shaven chin.

"Yes," was all she could manage to say. He wasn't exactly what could be termed handsome but his jaw was strong and his features fitted well together. She also noted that even without his thick coating of hair, he could still look bearishly grim.

"I'm on my to Guatemala in a few days. Being clean shaven is a lot more comfortable in that environment." He motioned toward the interior of her apartment. "Do you mind if I come in?"

"I was planning on spending a quiet evening *alone,*" she said pointedly, wondering why he was even there. She'd been certain he would never look her up again.

Ignoring the "get lost" tone in her voice, Peter brushed past her. Waiting until she closed the door and turned to face him, he said, "I came to apologize. Maybe I was a bit too cynical yesterday."

Refusing to think about the disquieting effect of his nearness as he'd entered, she breathed a disgruntled sigh. "Your apology might be premature."

Surprised, he raised an eyebrow questioningly.

She grimaced self-consciously and returned to her place on the couch.

She looked like she could use a friend, he thought. Then he noticed the diamond. It, coupled with her response to his apology, caused him to again call himself a fool. "Nice ring," he observed dryly.

"Yes." She'd been again staring at the stone. Now her eyes changed focus. He was standing where, without changing her line of vision, she could see his jeans-clad legs. A fire flamed to life within her. These bouts of lust she was experiencing were not helping her think clearly, she berated herself. They were also irrational. She and Peter Whitley were basically strangers. They didn't even like each other. She lifted her gaze to his face, expecting to see that his cynical expression had returned. It had, and the fire died.

She was just as mercenary as his ex-wife had been. So why did he still have the urge to protect her? Peter grumbled silently. "Decided you don't want to give it up?"

She frowned at him. "Do you have any idea how many women would like to be in my place? Charles is handsome, rich, and he adores me. Or at least that's what he claims."

"You left out the part where you're supposed to declare your love for him," Peter reminded her.

"That's the hard part." Tears of frustration welled in her eyes. "A week ago I was sure I was in love with him. Now all I seem to do is find fault with him. Today, for a little while I even thought of him as a bully."

His late encounter with Charles had remained too

sharp in Peter's mind for him to ignore it. "Has it ever occurred to you that maybe he is a bully?"

Her frown turned to a glare. "What I think is that I'm overreacting. I thought he was perfect. But that wasn't fair of me. No one is perfect. Now I'm being childish and making him out to be worse than he really is."

"Or maybe you're seeing him as he really is."

"You don't even know him. He's charming and well liked. He gives to charity and goes to church every Sunday."

"You're making him into a paragon again," Peter warned.

"I want a husband and a family. I'd be an idiot to turn down this opportunity."

Peter told himself she wanted to talk herself into marrying Charles, and he should let her do it. Charles's money could provide her with enough compensation for putting up with him. "I'd never classify you as an idiot."

She raked her hands through her hair and groaned. "I don't like to think I'm so shallow that I'd convince myself I was in love with Charles just because he's handsome, charming and wealthy. But if I really was in love with him, then that love wouldn't just die overnight. It must still be somewhere inside of me."

Watching her, Peter was forced to admit that he'd misjudged her. She really was in agony. "There is another possibility."

She looked up at him hopefully.

"Maybe you never knew the real Charles Tucker. Maybe finding him with another woman opened your eyes and now you're seeing a man you didn't know...the man beneath the charming exterior.''

She scowled at the diamond. ''Which makes me a naive, blind idiot.''

''Some people are very good at hiding their faults in order to get what they want.''

The underlying bitterness in his voice caused her gaze to level on him. ''Why do I get the impression you're speaking from experience?''

He shrugged. ''Probably because I am.''

Her gaze narrowed further. ''It was a woman, wasn't it?''

''My wife.''

''Your wife? The stoic, insular Peter Whitley actually took a wife?'' Her flippant tone hid a disquieting sensation that felt very much like jealousy. Determinedly she ignored it.

''A more accurate description would be to say she took me.'' His eyes darkened like the sky before a storm. ''I thought she was in love with me. But her real love was money.''

Indignation spread over her features. ''So that's why you've been so cynical about my feelings for Charles. Your wife left you for a wealthy man, and now you think all women can be bought.''

''The world can be a very mercenary place.''

''From your point of view,'' she retorted. Then the sparkle from the diamond recaptured her attention, and she sighed. ''Maybe mine, too. Maybe I want to be in love with Charles because I don't want to give up the life he can give me.''

Peter pictured her married to Charles. A sour taste came into his mouth. ''I've learned that it's always wise to take a close look at the path ahead before treading down it.''

''On the other hand, he who hesitates is lost,'' she returned tiredly. Looking up at him, she again wondered what it would be like to be kissed fully on the lips by him. Angry that this thought was still tormenting her, she started to shove it out of her mind, then stopped. ''Would you kiss me?'' she asked bluntly.

Peter didn't want to admit how much he hungered to do just that. *The woman is in a confused state of mind,* he reminded himself for the umpteenth time. Getting involved with her would only mean trouble. ''I'm not so sure that's such a good idea.''

''Maybe not,'' she admitted. ''But I'm desperate. It's been a long time since I kissed anyone but Charles. I want something to compare with his kiss.'' The notion sounded silly, now that she'd said it aloud. And Peter's hesitation convinced her he wasn't interested. An embarrassed flush began to spread upward from her neck. ''Forget I asked.''

Keep your distance, he ordered himself, but he wasn't listening. The pout on her face was making her lips look even more enticing. ''The experts say a person should always comparison shop.'' Approaching the couch, he captured her by the upper arms and lifted her to her feet.

His hands burned their imprint into her. Their strength tantalized while their heat spread through her like a river of fire. Reaching her womanly core, it ignited the flames of passion. Disbelief at the magnitude of her reaction shook her. He had not even begun the kiss and already her body was beginning to feel like molten lava.

Then his mouth found hers. The world around her vanished. All that was left was him. As he drew her into his embrace, bringing their bodies into contact, her entire awareness was focused on him. Wanting...no needing...a more complete contact, she parted his coat pushing aside the heavy fabric denying her access to the man beneath. Her legs weakened as he pulled her harder against him. The coaxing warmth of his mouth invited her to deepen the kiss, and she did.

Peter had never wanted to bed a woman more. The taste of her...the feel of her...aroused him with a strength that threatened his control.

Ellen felt his maleness hard against her, and she ached to offer it harbor. Even Charles had never aroused her desire to such heights. She could barely think, and what she was thinking was not rational...not for her. She knew she should stop, but she didn't want to. She wanted this ecstasy to continue forever.

She'll hate you in the morning, Peter's inner voice yelled at him as his hands slid beneath the fabric of her sweatpants. *But she started this,* he argued back.

Ellen trembled as his touch became more intimate. She'd never allowed Charles this much liberty, and yet she was encouraging it from Peter...a man with whom she knew she had no future. After all these years of waiting, to give herself to someone who would never marry her was insane, her rational mind shouted at her. It was right. She knew it was right. "We have to stop," she choked out, pushing away from him.

For a moment he continued to hold her, then as the panic in her voice reached his brain, he released her and stepped back.

"I'm sorry," she apologized shakily. "I never

meant...I never thought...you...me. We don't even like each other. You think I'm mercenary. I think you're a self-righteous boor."

"Could be we've both judged each other too harshly." With the taste and feel of her still lingering on and in him, he tried to clear his mind enough to think beyond his lust.

Her legs too weak to support her, she sank down onto the couch. "This proves my emotions and my body can't be trusted." Tears of frustration filled her eyes. "I never had any trouble stopping myself before. But I actually wanted to be intimate with you." She looked up at him. "That's nuts! You don't want to marry me, and I don't want to marry you."

"We could both do worse," he heard himself saying.

Surprised that he hadn't agreed with her, she looked up to find him studying her from behind a shuttered mask. The image of him waiting for her at the end of the aisle, played through her mind. To her amazement it not only looked right but felt right. "I thought..."

He read the spark of interest in her eyes and considered suggesting that they take some time and get to know each other better, then scowled at this notion. He'd made one mistake, he had no intention of making another. "Your problem is that you're not thinking rationally right now," he said curtly, more for his own ears than for hers. "You're on the rebound. It'd be best if we both forgot this ever happened."

Before she could respond, he strode out of the apartment and out of the building. Standing in the cold night air, he took several deep breaths to aid him in regaining control of his body and his sanity. He told himself he'd done the right thing by leaving when he had. But it wasn't the right thing if he'd thrown her back into Charles Tucker's clutches, his conscience rebutted. The Tuckers weren't good enough for her.

"I'm thinking like a man in love," he grumbled at himself as he climbed into his car. Ellen was in a vulnerable state. If he pursued her, he had a chance of winning her. But eventually, she'd get over the shock of Charles's betrayal and regret having married on the rebound. The frown on his face deepened. But if she married Tucker, she'd be just as miserable. Of that he was certain. "Or, maybe that's what I want to believe." His expression darkening even more, he drove back to Ian's place.

Ellen watched Peter pulling out of the parking lot. That was twice now that he'd inspired wanton behavior in her. As he drove away, instead of feeling relieved that he was gone, she felt as if a part of her was leaving with him.

"He's right. I'm not thinking straight," she muttered, leaving the window and returning to the couch.

Peter Whitley was nothing more than a fanciful adventure. A diversion from the hurt of Charles's betrayal. Lucky for her he was a man of conscience. And compassion, she added again recalling their rescue of the Pyresses. And now that she knew about his ex-wife, she could even understand the accusations he'd flung at her.

Grimacing ruefully, she admitted that he was basically a good man, then noted that this was the one bright spot in her day. It was nice to know she hadn't lusted after a heel.

Her grimace turned to a frown. "Thinking about Peter Whitley is not going to solve my problem."

She tried to again focus her thoughts on Charles but Peter's image persisted, rekindling the fires of desire.

"I'm so confused!" she wailed. Grabbing up a throw pillow, she buried her face in it to muffle a frustrated scream.

The phone rang, and she lifted her head just enough to look at it with one eye. It rang again. Deciding to let the answering machine pick it up, she waited. The caller was her mother. Feeling guilty about avoiding her own mother, she lifted the receiver. "Hi, Mom."

"You're there." Concern was strong in Ruth Reese's voice. "Since you're waiting to see who's calling, can I assume you and Charles have not mended your fences as yet?"

"Not yet."

"Well, you've always done what you wanted to do. I just hope you realize how much you're giving up if you break your engagement. And I'm not just talking about the kind of life he can provide for you. He's a charming, kind man. That woman probably threw herself at him."

"He claims that's what happened," Ellen admitted.

Triumph sounded in her mother's voice. "I thought so."

"So what about the next woman who throws herself at him?"

"Well, the next time you'll be sharing his bed, and you can just see that he's kept satisfied at home. In fact, I'm sending you a couple of books I found at the bookstore today. It can't hurt for you to do a little research before your wedding night."

The less-than-subtle pressure her mother was applying grated on Ellen's nerves, but she knew that her mother honestly wanted what was best for her. The thought of the very prim and proper Ruth Reese looking through sex manuals brought a wry smile to Ellen's face. "Thanks, Mom," she said, admitting that she had been feeling insecure about her knowledge regarding intimacy and was planning to do some reading before she walked down the aisle. Suddenly, it occurred to her that in Peter's arms she hadn't felt any need for guidance.

"I know you probably think I'm interfering too much, but I just don't want to see you make a decision you'll regret," Ruth continued in a rush. "Charles loves you."

A sudden realization dawned on Ellen. "He called you."

"He was worried that you might do something rash. He mentioned that Mr. Whitley had pursued you to Boston."

"Mr. Whitley is not pursuing me, and I'm not going to do anything rash," Ellen assured her.

"I'm relieved to hear that. Living in a mountain cabin with a wolf is not the kind of life I pictured for you." Ruth breathed a wistful sigh. "Charles has such a nice house. And servants. Your children would have all the advantages. And I know you wouldn't have agreed to marry him if you didn't love him. You're just hurt and angry right now. That's normal. To throw all of that away because of one indiscretion would be a shame."

Ellen knew her mother wasn't as mercenary as she sounded. Her parents had started out life with nothing. Her father had been employed as a mechanic at the local gas station, and her mother had worked at the grocery to make ends meet. But her mother had never complained about the hardships of those early years. They hadn't had many of life's luxuries, but they'd been a happy family. Now her father owned the gas station and her mother did his books. It was a decent living.

It was, however, a pittance compared to Charles's income. When her parents had come to visit and saw the extent of the Tuckers' wealth, they'd been intimidated by it, then awed at the prospect of their daughter sharing in that lifestyle. When Ellen and Charles had announced their engagement, her mother had been ecstatic. She'd seen a wonderful future ahead for her daughter. And Ellen admitted seeing that, as well.

"I appreciate you calling, but I'm really too tired to talk about this anymore right now," Ellen said politely but firmly. She was having a hard enough time sorting out her feelings on her own. She didn't need any pressure from anyone...even someone with her best interests at heart. After a few more guarantees to her mother that she wouldn't do anything rash, she hung up and returned her attention to the ring. She recalled how much she'd been looking forward to life with Charles. Leaning back, she closed her eyes. To her chagrin, it was the cabin that entered her mind.

Scowling, she opened her eyes and sat up rigidly. So Peter Whitley brought out the animal lust in her. A marriage couldn't survive on that alone. Besides, he was most likely right about her reactions to him being a rebound response to her disappointment with Charles. And he definitely wasn't what she wanted in a husband. As far as she knew he didn't even have a place to call home.

"I can't believe I'm even thinking about him as a

possible mate,'' she growled. She'd always been a sane, rational, practical person. "He's totally unsuitable for me.''

She ordered him out of her head, but he refused to go. "I'll settle this problem once and for all,'' she declared, rising from the couch and going in search of the phone book.

"I assume you've had contact with Miss Reese again.''

Peter looked up from the chart in front of him to see Ian watching him with an amused gleam in his eyes. "What caused you to draw that conclusion?''

"You came in. Barely said a word to me. Took out those charts and started through them like you'd had an inspiration. Then suddenly you came to a halt, and for the past fifteen minutes you've been staring at the same spot in something resembling a catatonic state,'' Ian elaborated.

Peter straightened. For a moment he remained silent, then said, "I find my attraction to the woman growing steadily.''

"I'd surmised as much. I've never seen you so on edge.''

Peter frowned at himself. "I apologize if I've been unpleasant company.''

"No. No. You haven't been unpleasant. You've provided an interesting diversion. I've been wondering how long it would be before you admitted the real reason you followed Miss Reese to Boston.''

"I did tell you the real reason. I'm not here to court her. I don't want a wife who will wake up one morning, look at me and exclaim, 'How did I get here?' then accuse me of taking advantage of her in a weakened state.''

Ian smiled. "I'll let you in on a little secret. No matter what the circumstances are when you wed, there will be mornings when your wife wakes up and wonders why she married you. And there will be mornings when you wake up and wonder why you married her. It's part of the human condition. You get over those bumps in the rocky road of life and go on together.''

"Not if she married you on the rebound and suddenly realizes she doesn't love you...that you were merely a crutch to get past her hurt and anger."

"Perhaps," Ian conceded.

A sharp knock on the door interrupted them.

Answering it, Ian smiled with interest at the woman on his doorstep.

"Professor Cochran?" Ellen asked, then added quickly. "I'm Ellen Reese. I need to speak to Peter Whitley."

"Yes. Of course you are, and of course you do." Stepping aside, he motioned for her to enter.

"I apologize for coming so late," she said, accepting his invitation.

Ian's smile broadened. "No need to do that. To be honest, I've been wanting to meet you."

Wondering what Peter had said about her to the professor, a flush of embarrassment reddened her cheeks. It doesn't matter, she told herself. She'd come for a purpose and that was all she needed to concern herself with.

"Peter is in the living room." Ian motioned toward an open door.

Striding into the room he'd indicated, she saw the

surprise on Peter's face. "I want to know a few things about you," she said curtly.

His surprise was replaced by a guarded expression. "What do you want to know?"

"You live a vagabond's existence, don't you? I'll bet you don't have a home anywhere...a house, a cave, anyplace you can hang your hat that is actually yours."

"As a matter of fact, I do," he replied evenly.

That wasn't the answer she expected or wanted. She'd come here to get the man out of her system. Skepticism showed on her face. "A cave?"

He couldn't stop himself from grinning. "No. It's a house."

The boyish amusement in his eyes caused her knees to weaken, and the frustration that had been building within her took control. "Don't you smile at me, Mr. Peter Whitley! You had no right to come barging into my life, complicating it even more than it already was."

His grin vanished. "I wasn't the one who barged into your life. You were the one who showed up on my doorstep. If anyone in this room can be accused of throwing a wrench into someone else's life, it's you throwing one into mine."

"Well, I don't recalling asking you to come to Boston," she countered hotly.

"You have a point," he conceded.

She frowned at herself. She hadn't come here to argue with him. All she wanted was information. "About your house, it's probably in some forsaken place no one ever goes, isn't it?"

"It's secluded."

"I knew it! A cabin in the woods just like the one in New Hampshire only maybe more primitive." She continued to glare at him. "And you probably don't have a steady job, either, do you? You just live off the kindness of friends and only work when you have to."

He scowled at this accusation. "I have my own consulting firm and enough business to make ends meet."

She flushed with embarrassment. "Okay. So I'm sorry, I insinuated you were a freeloader."

He continued to study her guardedly. "Do you want to tell me what this is all about?"

"No." Her glare returned. "You did tell me once you traveled a lot?"

"My work requires that."

"So, it's safe to say that you're almost never at your home, wherever home is."

"Yes, it's safe to say that."

"I knew it!" Triumph showed on her face. "You're not suitable husband material...at least, not for me. And it's my guess your first wife probably didn't leave you because she found a wealthy husband. She left you because you were never around. Well, that's not the kind of life I want." Turning sharply, she headed for the front door. Passing Professor Cochran, who was standing just inside the room, she said, "Thank you and, again, I apologize for interrupting your evening."

"Thank you for coming," he said, following her to the door. "You livened up the evening."

Her cheeks reddened again and she quickly exited the town house. Climbing into her car, she told herself that she didn't care that she'd created a scene. She had the answers she needed. Now she could go home and make a sane, adult decision about the rest of her life.

Ian chuckled as he closed the door. Turning to find Peter standing in the doorway of the living room, he said, "That woman has fire. I like her. And I think it's a safe bet that she's attracted to you." His tone changed to one of fatherly reprimand. "You could have painted a more appealing picture of your lifestyle."

"I answered her honestly," Peter replied. "My work does take me all over the world."

"But you could have mentioned that she could come with you...travel romantic byways and see fascinating sights. She might even be a help. You're always complaining about machinery breaking down. You told me that she's a mechanical engineer. Maybe she could develop some better designs."

Peter scowled. "Under other circumstances, I would have tried to convince her to give me a chance. You're right, there is a strong physical attraction between us, but it's obvious she's fighting it tooth and nail. She wants the life Charles Tucker would give her...country club, parties...elegant balls. She came here looking for reasons to discredit me."

"She did seem bent on convincing herself that you were not for her," Ian admitted. "But she wouldn't have to do that if the possibility of marrying you hadn't crossed her mind."

"I've already told you she's confused. I will not take advantage of a woman in her condition. We'd both live to regret it."

"It's my opinion that if you pursued Miss Reese and won her away from Mr. Tucker, you would be saving her from a fate she might regret even more. She would be much better off waking up in your bed and wondering how she got there than waking up to some unpleasant truth in his," Ian argued. His expression grew grim.

"And just now you could very easily have helped her convince herself that she should marry the man."

Peter had to admit he didn't like that possibility.

Back in her apartment, Ellen sat on her couch and shoved the ring onto her finger. Marrying Charles was the right decision for her. Her mother thought so, and Charles had promised to be faithful. As for her cynical view of him today, that was an unfair evaluation brought on by residual anger. He was the boss. He had to rule with a firm hand. And if he wanted to take advantage of his position once in a while, then he had a right.

The ring felt heavy, and her resolve wavered. "Don't be a fool," she admonished herself, and left it on.

Chapter Ten

Ellen sat at her breakfast table the next morning staring into a cup of strong, black coffee. All night long she'd dreamed. Most were only vague undefinable shadows in the recesses of her mind. But one wasn't. In that one she'd been in Peter's arms. Her body had seemed to sing with joy, then suddenly he was gone, replaced by Charles. She'd woken feeling chilled and unhappy.

"I don't believe in love at first sight," she informed the dark liquid. "What I feel for Peter Whitley is lust at first sight. It won't last."

But the thought that while it did last, it could be extraordinarily enjoyable refused to be dismissed. "What has happened to the sane, rational me...the woman who knew what she wanted in life?"

Her gaze shifted to the ring on her finger. "She's still here and on her way to achieving her goal." The words sounded like a lie.

The ringing of the phone caused her to jump slightly.

"Hello, dear," her mother's voice came over the line. "I've been worrying about you all night."

"Mom, do you believe in love at first sight?" she asked tiredly.

"Well, I will admit I knew from the first time I saw your father that he was the man for me. He was seven, and I was five. Of course we had a lot of years to get to know each other, and I knew what kind of man he was by the time I married him." Panic laced the concern in Ruth's voice. "We aren't talking about you and that Peter Whitley, are we?"

"He does stir up some very strong emotions," Ellen admitted.

"It's just a rebound reaction or wild oats. You've never sown any wild oats. And it would only be natural for you to still be angry with Charles. Getting involved with Peter Whitley might be your way of getting back at him. But I don't think that's such a good idea." The worry in her mother's voice deepened. "You haven't done anything foolish, have you? You're not already involved with him, are you?"

"No." Ellen experienced a sharp jab of regret.

Ruth's tone became stern. "Consider each path available to you and picture your life five years from now."

Ellen knew her mother was being practical, but her nerves were brittle this morning and she heard herself saying dryly, "I could be dead five years from now."

"Precisely! And what if you've had a child or even two by then. You know Charles could give them a good life. But what about Mr. Whitley? Do you think he could raise them on his own?"

"You have a point," Ellen admitted. Her head was

beginning to pound. "I need to get dressed for work. Don't worry, I won't do anything rash."

"I'm only concerned about what's best for you," Ruth said again before hanging up.

As she dressed, Ellen considered her mother's words. She recalled how Charles had looked posing with a couple of children during one of the many charity functions his mother had organized. He'd appeared cool and aloof, and she'd had the feeling that he'd rather have been doing anything other than holding that baby. "It's normal for men to be uneasy around small children. He'll be different with his own," she assured herself.

Suddenly she was recalling how good Peter had been with Philip and how natural he'd looked holding the boy.

"Peter Whitley isn't the least bit interested in a wife and family," she grumbled at herself. And even if he was, after last night she wouldn't be a candidate. "Concentrate on Charles," she ordered herself.

Again her gaze went to the ring, and she remembered how excited she'd been when Charles had first slipped it on her finger. A glance at her watch told her it was time to leave for the plant. Taking the ring off, she placed it in the jeweler's box for safekeeping and started out of the room. Before reaching the door, she came to a halt. Retracing her steps, she returned, took the ring out of the box, put it on her finger and the box in her pocket. She'd decided to marry Charles and she would wear his ring wherever safety regulations allowed.

Entering her office, she found a note from him. It informed her that he had business meetings all day but that he would pick her up for dinner at seven. Relief that she had a few hours before seeing him swept through her. She needed a little more time to get her thinking straightened out and back on a reasonable, rational path.

Going down the hall, she knocked on Paul's door.

He barked a gruff "Enter."

"I want to apologize for yesterday afternoon. I didn't mean to leave you shorthanded," she said apologetically.

He shrugged. "We missed you, but we got along just fine." Appearing more relaxed than she'd seen him in a long time, he nodded toward a stack of papers on his desk. "I could use your help going through these applications."

"We're hiring again?" she asked in surprise.

"Charles wants your position filled before the wedding."

Ellen recalled that Charles had mentioned something about her quitting work and becoming a full-time wife, but she hadn't agreed yet. Of course she would. Yesterday had opened her eyes to the strain Paul was under being her superior. Besides, she had to admit that she was becoming bored with her job. She preferred something that required more creativity than choosing a pump or motor. Designing the pump or motor was more appealing, or even simply fixing them. Wistfully she recalled how much she enjoyed actual hands-on work and how triumphant she felt when she got a machine running once again. After the wedding, she could turn a corner of Charles's four-car garage into a workshop and concentrate on a few designs of her own. Still, it irked her that he'd made the decision without even consulting her.

He's simply trying to keep the company running

smoothly, she reasoned. While the excitement of being courted in royal fashion had blinded her to Paul's growing discomfort in her presence, Charles had probably been aware of it for some time. "I'll be happy to help," she said.

"Take them back to your office. Go through them and give me a list in order of your preference. Then we'll start arranging interviews," Paul instructed.

Charles was apparently very positive he would win her back, she mused as she picked up the files. Well, he was a confident man. In the past she'd admired that trait. It wasn't fair to hold it against him now. Besides, he was right, she added catching a glint of sparkle from the diamond on her finger. An uneasiness rippled through her. Determinedly she ignored it. She'd made the right decision!

She'd gone through the folders, arranged them in order of her preference and was working on a report concerning the pros and cons of the two motors she'd been trying to decide between for the new production line when there was a knock on her door and Loretta Tucker entered.

"I've come to take you to lunch," the woman said. Her gaze fastened on Ellen's hand. "So you've decided to marry my son, after all. How lovely. We can spend the meal discussing plans for the wedding."

Ellen smiled weakly. "I'm not certain I'm ready for that."

Loretta's smile became motherly. "It's never too soon to begin. Come along."

Continuing to force a smile, Ellen turned off her computer and grabbed her coat and purse. She wasn't really in the mood to go to lunch with Loretta, but she didn't want to offend her future mother-in-law.

"I've made reservations at the country club," Loretta said on their way to the front door. As they pulled away in the chauffeured limousine, she opened the small refrigerator. "I'm sorry I don't have any champagne to toast your decision to marry Charles but there is some wine."

"I need to keep a clear head for work this afternoon," Ellen refused politely.

Loretta pouted. "Too bad." Her smile returning, she poured herself a glass, raised it in salute to Ellen, then took a large swallow. "I'm so pleased for you and Charles. This is going to make our luncheon much more enjoyable. The truth is, I was feeling guilty about not pleading my son's case. Now I won't have to. We can get on with the business of planning your big day."

Although Ellen had assured herself a zillion times during the past hours that marrying Charles was the right and rational thing to do, Loretta's insistence on making plans for the wedding was causing a fresh wave of anxiousness. *I'm simply experiencing the usual cold feet some people get before making a big commitment,* she reasoned. Still, she hadn't felt this reluctance before last Saturday night.

Peter Whitley again popped into her mind. She shoved him out.

At the club they were led to a secluded table in a windowed alcove.

"I'll have champagne. The best you have in stock," Loretta told the waiter when he approached. "And pop the cork before you bring the bottle. I hate drawing attention to myself.'' She looked to Ellen. ''Are you sure you won't join me?''

''I'll just have coffee,'' Ellen replied. ''I really do have to work this afternoon.''

As the waiter hurried away, Loretta smiled knowingly. ''You'll learn to like champagne any time of day. Indulging in the finer things is what makes life palatable.''

Ellen was surprised by this remark. She'd always thought of Loretta as being happy and content.

Loretta glanced at the menu. ''The salmon is delicious.''

''Sounds lovely,'' Ellen replied, not in any mood to peruse the menu herself. She'd seen it before. Most of it was in French and there were no prices. ''If you have to ask the cost, you didn't belong here,'' Charles had told her. At the time she'd been impressed. Now that remark sounded elitist and grated on her nerves.

Loretta's champagne came. She downed the first glass while they placed their luncheon orders. The waiter poured her another before leaving their table.

Remembering the wine the woman had drunk in the limo, Ellen began to feel uncomfortable. She'd never seen Loretta drink more than one glass of anything before.

''I promised my husband and son I wouldn't drink too much in public,'' Loretta confided as she downed the second glass and poured herself a third. ''But I had a restless night, and besides you're not 'public,' you're practically family.''

The thought of explaining to Charles that she'd allowed his mother to get drunk at lunch didn't appeal to

Ellen. "Maybe you should switch to coffee," she suggested.

Loretta held up a hand as if to say don't worry. "I just needed a couple of glasses to relax. I'll sip this next one. I promise."

It's a good thing she's using the limo and not driving herself today, Ellen thought.

Loretta leaned closer and lowered her voice. "Charles refused to tell me what you argued about, but my guess is that it was another woman."

Ellen shifted uncomfortably as she again recalled Janet coming down the stairs in Charles's shirt.

Loretta grinned conspiratorially. "I thought so."

Feeling guilty for having divulged a secret Charles had obviously not wanted his mother to share, Ellen said quickly, "He has promised it will never happen again."

Loretta patted her hand. "And of course you believe him."

The patronizing tone in the older woman's voice increased Ellen's uneasiness. "Are you suggesting that I'm being naive?"

"My dear, being naive would be to give all of this up—" Loretta paused to make a sweeping gesture with her arm toward the interior of the elegant dining room and then the marina beyond the wall of windows "—just because your husband has a roving eye." She again lowered her voice and leaned close to Ellen. "The first time is always the hardest. But it gets easier. You simply learn to throw a fit and threaten divorce. He soothes you with an extremely extravagant gift, and you go on."

Ellen had heard vague rumors about Howard Tucker

and his philandering, but she hadn't believed them because Loretta had always seemed so calm and secure in her marriage. "I thought you and Howard were happy together."

"We are." Loretta smiled slyly. "He plays his games and I play mine. I like to think we're an even match. Of course, he thinks he's much more clever than me, and I let him think that. It gives me an advantage." She again patted Ellen's hand in a motherly manner. "You should keep that in mind. Play a little dumb so that others will underestimate you." She downed the third glass.

Ellen didn't like the picture the woman was painting. "I'm really glad you invited me to lunch," she said. "But I just remembered that there's something very important I have to take care of at the office."

Loretta suddenly flushed worriedly. "You won't mention our little talk to my son? He wouldn't like to know I gave you a few pointers." She covered her mouth with her hand to hide a belch. "And you won't mention the champagne, either, will you?"

"I won't mention any of this," Ellen promised. "And thank you again," she said sincerely.

Crossing the parking lot to her car, she took the ring off her finger and returned it to the jeweler's box. Loretta Tucker was willing to sell her soul for life's luxuries, but she was not.

Inside the dining room, Loretta sat with a thoughtful expression on her face.

"Will your companion be returning soon?" the waiter asked, returning with the food.

"I don't think so. I just gave her a dose of reality,

and I don't think she liked the taste of it." Loretta abruptly grinned. "And, now that I've performed my good deed for today, I deserve to celebrate. I'll have a glass of real champagne to wash the taste of that ginger ale out of my mouth."

"Yes, ma'am," the waiter replied with a matching grin.

Ellen left a message with Harriet that she wanted to see Charles before he left the plant. She knew she'd made the right decision this time. From the moment she'd seen Janet at Charles's house, she'd known that she would never be able to entirely trust him again.

During the remainder of the afternoon, she concentrated on the report she'd begun that morning. She was finishing when a knock sounded on her door and she looked up to see Charles enter.

"I hope you aren't going to cancel our dinner date because you have work to catch up on," he said, with his most charming, beseeching smile. "I can't have my employees depriving themselves of sustenance and collapsing on the job."

She rose to face him. "I am canceling our dinner date but not because of work. I can't marry you. I've tried to convince myself that I could learn to trust you again, but I can't."

His smile turned to a frown. "You're being unfair."

"Maybe," she agreed. "But I can't get the image of you and Janet out of my mind."

"It's that Neanderthal, Whitley, isn't it. He pursued you here, and you've discovered you prefer the caveman type."

"He is not a Neanderthal," she snapped, then was startled by how fervently she felt about defending Peter.

Charles sneered. "Really, Ellen, I thought you had better taste than that."

His insulting manner raised her ire. "This has nothing to do with Peter Whitley or my taste in men. It has to do with you and your inability to be faithful."

Charles's gaze turned cold. "It's obvious your mind is made up."

Taking the jeweler's box from her pocket, she extended it toward him. "Yes. I'm really sorry things have worked out this way."

He took the box from her and slipped it in his pocket. "I'll expect your desk to be cleaned out tonight. I'll have payroll cut you a check for three months' salary, and a messenger will bring it by your apartment tomorrow morning."

She stared at him in disbelief. "You're firing me?"

"I don't like reminders of my mistakes."

She couldn't believe her ears or her eyes. The Charles she knew was gone, replaced by a stranger with cold disdain etched into his face.

"If you want any kind of decent letters of recommendation, you'll leave without protest," he finished.

Ellen recalled Janet packing for California and wondered if the woman had really wanted to leave town. "If you don't get your way, you just buy the person off?" She felt as if she was seeing the real Charles for the first time. He reminded her of a spoiled child. "I thought you honestly cared for me."

"That was what attracted me to you…your naiveté and innocence." He smirked. "I always feel challenged to initiate virgins into the world of erotic sensation. Normally I would have simply seduced you. But you were determined to stick to your principles. Besides, my father felt it was time I married and started a family, and I agreed with him. And you seemed like the perfect choice. You were intelligent, pretty but not so glamorous I'd have to worry about other men. You wanted a home and children, and you seemed reasonably easy to manipulate. I was wrong. I want you out tonight.''

"You never loved me."

He shrugged. "I liked you. That's more than I can say about most people."

"The charming, caring, considerate man I thought I knew was all a facade," she muttered.

"As Shakespeare once said, 'Life's a stage and we are all actors' or something to that effect." He started to leave, but paused with his hand on the knob. "You will tell everyone that ours was an amiable parting. If you don't, you will not receive any severance pay, and I will inform any employer who seeks a recommendation that you are a troublemaker and inadequate at your job."

Ellen had been studying this stranger in front of her with a fresh eye. "There is one thing that puzzles me," she said before he could open the door.

He turned back. "I thought I'd made my position perfectly clear."

"You have and it's obvious you're not the forgiving type. So, if I had had an affair with Peter Whitley, why were you so willing to overlook it?" An answer crossed her mind. "Were you planning to toss it in my face each time you had an affair and I found out about it?"

"Nothing so mundane as that. If you hadn't convinced me that you hadn't allowed that uncouth clod to bed you, I'd have wooed you back and then dropped you like a hot potato."

Understanding spread over her face. "So that I could be the one who was jilted."

"Precisely."

Ellen watched in silence as he left. At least she'd discovered the real Charles Tucker before she'd married him.

Going down to shipping, she found some boxes. Paul was in his office when she passed on her way back. Retrieving the folders from her desk, she carried them down to him. "I'm quitting," she said simply, placing them in front of him. "I've arranged these in order of who I think would best fit in here."

His gaze traveled from her taut features to her ringless finger. "You broke off your engagement with Charles?"

"It was a mutual decision," she replied stiffly. She wanted to add that she felt relieved to have discovered what a rat their boss was, but held back. She had no doubt Charles would keep his word about wrecking her chances of finding another job.

Paul's expression became fatherly. "It's better to find out you're not suited to each other before the vows are said than after."

"You're right about that," she replied.

He smiled a comradely smile, and she could see in his eyes that he knew what a heel Charles could be.

She smiled back. Then returning to her office, she packed her things.

Paul came down a few minutes later and offered to help her carry her stuff to her car. As she drove away from the plant, she saw Loretta's limousine pulling in. She owed the woman a debt of gratitude.

Loretta found her son in his office, glaring out the window. "I ran into Paul on my way in. He told me that Ellen has quit."

Charles turned to her. "She decided she didn't want to marry me, and I decided I didn't want her around."

"Just like one of your toys when it got busted or you got bored with it," Loretta mused.

He frowned at her. "I was fair. I gave her three months' severance pay, and I'll see that she gets excellent letters of recommendation."

"You're right. That's very fair," Loretta conceded, seating herself in one of the winged leather chairs fronting his desk.

A sneer spread over his face. "She said that Neanderthal, Whitley, had nothing to do with her decision, but I'll bet it did. She probably thinks living in a cave will be romantic."

"Perhaps," Loretta agreed.

"Well they're welcome to each other."

"I'm sure she'll get what she deserves," Loretta soothed.

Charles eyed his mother suspiciously. "I thought you liked Ellen."

"I do. But she's clearly not the woman for you. You need someone who can be bought, like me."

Charles frowned. "You know I hate your introspective moods. I hope you're not going to get morose."

"I'm not and I'm not being introspective, just honest. I've accepted my life as it is and am reasonably happy with it. You know what they say...money can't buy happiness but it can buy you a much more luxurious level of misery."

"You've been drinking," he accused with disdain.

"No, I haven't. I just had one glass of wine and one glass of champagne several hours ago." Loretta eased herself to her feet. "But I did spend the afternoon in a boring planning meeting for next month's charity ball. So you can be a dear and take me someplace nice for dinner. Just make certain it's not where your father is taking his latest bimbette."

"If you promise to behave and have no more to drink," Charles bargained.

"Promise," she replied, slipping her arm though his.

Chapter Eleven

Ellen studied the map of the United States. "Where do I want to work?" she mused. She'd already determined that she would leave Boston. The further she was from Charles Tucker, the better she'd like it. And Kansas City was out. This was not the time to live anywhere near her parents. Her broken engagement was bound to send her mother into a matchmaking frenzy, and she didn't want to deal with that.

"At least I'll be leaving here without any regrets," she added, glad that she'd stood by her principles and hadn't surrendered her virginity to Charles Tucker. To have given herself wholly to him and then discovered he was a heel would have been devastating.

Still, a nagging sense of disappointment persisted. But it had nothing to do with Charles. It had to do with Peter Whitley. "We're totally unsuited for each other," she grumbled at herself. She wanted a home. Being settled in one spot wasn't his style. The only thing they had in common was a lust for each other. "After last night, he's never going to want to see me again anyway and that's for the best." Her jaw stiffened. "I need to put the past several days behind me and get on with my life."

A knock on her door surprised her. Long hours at work had prevented her from making any close friends. There were a couple of other single women in her apartment complex with whom she'd gone to dinner and the movies a couple of times but after she'd started dating Charles, he'd taken up all of her spare time. A horrible thought suddenly crossed her mind. What if her mother had decided to come to see for herself what was going on here?

"Maybe it's Karen from down the hall needing to borrow a couple of eggs," she murmured hopefully under her breath.

Opening the door, she stood mutely wondering if she was seeing things.

"Evening," Peter said, breaking the silence between them.

His presence caused a rush of pleasure. "I figured after last night you wouldn't want to have anything to do with me," she blurted out, still finding it hard to believe he was there. Then she saw the cold purpose in his eyes and the pleasure died. He was a man on a mission...one he did not expect her to like.

"You had your say. I decided I should have mine." He strode in, forcing her to take a couple of steps back or be collided with. Once inside he gave the door a shove to close it. She looked different, he thought. Less strained. The worry that he was too late—that she'd made up her mind to marry Charles or even worse, given herself completely to the man, raced through his mind. His jaw stiffened into an even harder line.

Ellen braced herself. After the insults she'd thrown at him, she deserved whatever he chose to toss her way. "I suppose you're here to tell me that in your book, I'm not acceptable wife material. Well..."

"That's not what I came to say." He stopped himself before he added that he thought she was excellent wife material. She was, but not for him. "You're right about me. I wouldn't fit into your concept of a good husband. I don't lead a settled life. Even more, I'd want any wife of mine to share my life with me. That'd mean sometimes living in tents in remote areas without any luxuries, with insects the size of your fingers and poisonous snakes."

Instead of begin repulsed by the picture he painted, Ellen found herself intrigued. She wasn't particularly fond of the idea of the snakes and insects. However, being with him in a tent did have its appeal.

"But my qualifications as a husband aren't important. Charles Tucker's are and, in my opinion, he isn't any better husband material than I am. If you're smart you'll take a close look at the guy before you cast your lot with his," Peter finished curtly.

Again she found herself thinking that she'd never seen eyes so blue. "You're right about Charles."

Relief spread through Peter. "So you've decided not to marry him."

"Yes, and I doubt our paths will ever cross again." She nodded toward the boxes in one corner of her living room. "He fired me."

"He fired you just because you wouldn't marry

him?'' The man was even more of a lowlife than he'd suspected, Peter mused.

"I'd appreciate it if you wouldn't tell anyone that,'' she said stiffly, fighting back a rush of embarrassment. It was bad enough admitting that she'd been duped by Charles, but that she'd capitulated to his demands caused an added jab of humiliation. "As long as I don't make any noise about what really happened, he'll give me three months' severance pay and glowing recommendations.''

Peter frowned. "You're letting him buy you off?''

She glared at him. "I'm being practical. I want to get as far away from him as possible, and I need the money and recommendations to get started elsewhere. Besides who would care, other than a few gossips, and it'd be old news in a couple of days. He could probably even turn the gossip to his advantage. He could say he found out I was gold digger. You thought that.''

Peter shrugged. "You've got a point." His mission was accomplished. It was time for him to leave and get on with his life. "Good luck," he said.

Watching him reach for the doorknob, and knowing that once he was gone she'd never see him again, caused Ellen a deep stab of regret. "You couldn't use a mechanical engineer in your company, could you? Or even just a good mechanic?'' Mentally she gasped at her forwardness.

For a moment he hesitated. Walking away from her was one of the hardest things he'd ever done. But it was the honorable thing to do, he told himself for the umpteenth time. "I don't think it's a good idea for me to hire you. I can't deny that I find you appealing...very appealing. I'm not so sure I could keep my distance, and you've just come out of a bad relationship. You're vulnerable. I wouldn't want something to happen between us we'd both regret.''

She knew he was right. She should be feeling very cautious where men were concerned. Yet, at this moment, the urge to kiss the corners of his mouth until she'd turned them from a frown to a soft smile was strong. This kind of behavior wasn't like her. Her rational side told her she shouldn't trust it. ''My mother thinks you're my version of 'sowing wild oats.''' She flushed when she realized she'd spoken aloud.

He grinned crookedly. ''Wild oats?''

''I never did sow any. Maybe that was a mistake.''

His expression became serious. ''I don't think so. You stuck by your principles. I admire you for that.'' She looked so wistful, the urge to take her in his arms was close to overwhelming. But he was certain that this time he wouldn't be able to stop if he felt her yielding once again. Taking out his wallet, he extracted a business card. ''I'm leaving for Guatemala in the next day or two. When you get settled, write me at the address on that card and let me know where you are. I'll come see you when I get back. If the attraction is still there, we'll know it's more than sowing wild oats or a rebound.''

''That is the practical way to handle this,'' she said, accepting the card. The address was a post office box in a town in Oregon. Mentally she mocked herself. He wanted her out of his life as much as Charles wanted her out of his. And this was a polite way of doing it. Her shoulders straightened with pride. ''My emotions are pretty much in a muddle right now. We, most likely, are totally incompatible. By the time you return we'll both be wondering how we could have found each other appealing.''

''Write me,'' he ordered, and left before his will broke and he reached for her.

Her chin trembled as the door closed behind him. His abrupt exit convinced her that he was as gone from her life as Charles was. But unlike her parting from Charles, this one hurt. Fighting back threatening tears, she chided herself for overreacting. She and Peter Whitley had known each other for less than a week. And they'd fought during most of that time. It should be obvious they were both better off going their separate ways.

She dropped the card in the trash. She wouldn't write. The smartest thing she could do was to put the past days entirely out of her mind.

Outside, Peter stood indecisively beside his car. Then his jaw tensed with resolve. Striding back inside the building, he knocked on Ellen's door. When she opened it, he entered and kicked it closed behind him. ''Marry me,'' he demanded.

Ellen stared at him in stunned silence. Certain she was imagining this entire thing, she closed her eyes, then opened them. He was still there. The words to accept his demand formed on the tip of her tongue, but instead she heard herself asking, ''What if we find out we really are incompatible?''

''I'd rather you woke up next to me, wondering why you were there, than decide to sow some wild oats or rebound into the arms of someone who would simply use you and discard you.''

''I thought you didn't want to be burdened with me,'' she said, still finding this turn of events difficult to believe.

"I didn't want a relationship I figured wouldn't last. But most of the choices we make in this life are a gamble to some extent. So why should marriage be any different?" He was tempted to end this debate by tossing her over his shoulder and carrying her home with him. That she brought out such strong primitive urges shook him.

"This is nuts. You know that. I know that." She grimaced self-consciously. "But then I haven't been behaving entirely rationally, anyway, lately. If you're serious about this…" She paused to give him one last chance to change his mind.

"I am," he said firmly.

"Then, all right, I'll marry you." She expected to experience a rush of panic. Instead excitement filled her. *This could be the biggest mistake of your life,* her little voice warned. She ignored it.

Three days later Ellen walked down the aisle of the small church on the outskirts of Kansas City that she'd attended since childhood. She was wearing her grandmother's wedding gown and carrying a bouquet of daisies and forget-me-nots.

Peter's parents had flown in from Arizona. They, her parents and her aunt Mae and uncle George, who lived close by, were the only attendees. Her mother was her maid of honor, and Peter's father was his best man.

Since their arrival yesterday, Peter's parents had treated her kindly and politely, but she's seen the worried look in their eyes. It matched the one in her parents' eyes. Several times during the days preceding the wedding, she'd had to assure her parents that she wasn't getting married because she had to, but because she wanted to. She guessed Peter had been doing the same.

"Are you sure you want to go through with this?" her father whispered in her ear as they approached the altar.

She looked at Peter waiting ahead of her. A part of her was still protesting that this was crazy, but a stronger part didn't care. "Yes."

"Who gives this woman into marriage?" the minister asked, as she and her father came to a halt before him.

"Her mother and me," David Reese replied.

She heard the hesitation in his voice and saw the look that passed between him and the minister. Then she noticed the minister glance toward Peter's father, and John Whitley gave him a small nod. What was going on? she wondered.

She looked to Peter. His jaw was set in a grim line. A knot formed in the pit of her stomach. Had he decided he wanted to call off the wedding but was too much of a gentleman to embarrass her by leaving her standing at the altar? Was that why her father had asked her if she wanted to go through with the ceremony? Did everyone know but her?

She looked to her mother and then to his. Both women were sitting stiffly as if expecting trouble.

Her cheeks flushed with pride. If Peter wanted out, all he had to do was say so. She was preparing to tell him that when the minister spoke.

"I have known you, Ellen, since you were a child, and I've never known you to behave irrationally and without thought." His gaze shifted to take in Peter, as well. "And both of you are old enough to know your own minds. However a request has been made by both sets of parents and, because it was made with love and concern, I feel bound by conscience to honor it. Before we continue with this ceremony, I must ask if both of you are certain you want to go through with this union.''

Ellen met Peter's gaze squarely. ''You knew this was going to happen and didn't warn me?'' she asked accusingly.

''I didn't know until just a few minutes ago. I couldn't stop it.'' The grim expression on his face grew grimmer. ''Besides, I wanted to see your reaction.''

''Or maybe you're having second thoughts and wanted an out,'' she said tersely.

The blue of his eyes darkened to the color of a midnight sky. ''I'm having no second thoughts. But if you are, I want to know now.''

She had expected to feel at least a little hesitant when the actual time came to exchange their vows. She didn't. ''I'm not having any second thoughts, either.''

Peter turned to the minister. ''Marry us,'' he ordered.

Now she was nervous, Ellen admitted. It was hours later. Following the ceremony, both sets of parents had apologized for insisting on one final declaration of intent and wished them well. Ellen and Peter had accepted their apologies gracefully. Neither doubted that their parents had acted out of love and concern. Then all had gone out to dinner to celebrate the nuptials. After which they'd gathered at her parents' house so that she could change into a suit and pick up her suitcase.

Now she and Peter were standing outside the door of the honeymoon suite at one of finest hotels in Kansas City. Since she'd had no one to toss her bouquet to, she'd kept it and was feigning interest in it while the bellhop opened the door and stepped aside.

In the next instant, everything but Peter was forgotten as he scooped her up in his arms and carried her across the threshold. When he set her on the floor and turned to take care of the bellhop, she frowned. The room was elegant, and she had no doubt it was expensive.

"I didn't expect anything so lavish," she said when they were alone. "If you did this to impress me, it wasn't necessary."

"I figured you deserved a bit of luxury. When we leave here, you're not going to find much," he replied, running his finger caressingly along the line of her jaw.

"I never expected any pampering." She marveled that the sentence had come out coherently. Just his light touch was causing the embers of desire to spark to life.

Taking the bouquet from her, he tossed it onto a nearby table. "Our plane leaves in less than forty-eight hours. I'd hate to waste any of that time with small talk."

"I'm not in the mood for small talk, either." She looked toward her suitcase. "I'll change for bed."

Peter considered letting her, but as she started to move away, his hand closed around her arm and he gently turned her back to him. "Why put on something I'll only be taking off?" Releasing her, he unbuttoned the jacket of her suit.

"Now that you mention it, that does seem like a worthless use of time." He was slipping the jacket off her now, and every fiber of her being was coming to life. As he tossed her jacket on the couch, she began to slip off his suit coat. She'd thought she would get nervous at this stage. Instead, her fingers sought the buttons of his shirt with unabashed purpose.

He let her discard it, then applied himself to finishing undressing her. Each touch, each brush of his hands heightened her senses until her body tingled with anticipation.

"I was sure being nude in front of a man would take some getting used to," she confessed as he kicked off his shoes. "Instead it seems natural...right."

His hands trailed over the curve of her hips. "You feel even better than I'd imagined."

The fire within her burned hotter, and she sought the button of his slacks. "I will admit you are a little intimidating," she confessed as she finished her task of undressing him.

"I'll try to go slowly," he vowed, lifting her in his arms and carrying her to the bed.

"Not too slowly," she said as she reached down and pulled back the covers.

"No, not too slowly," he replied gruffly, joining her on the satin sheets.

Then all conversation ceased as they became lost in a world of sensation.

Ellen frowned thoughtfully as she forked a bite of omelette into her mouth. They'd been in the hotel room for more than thirty-six hours with no contact with the outside world except for room service. By now she should be getting at least a little tired of their lovemaking. Instead, she was in a lazy haze of relaxed enjoyment.

"A penny for your thoughts," Peter offered from the other side of the table.

"I never really believed sex could be so thrilling," she admitted. Then laughed. "I also can't believe we aren't exhausted. Admittedly we've napped a little, but not much."

"I, for one, am feeling a little tired," he told her with a grin.

A flush reddened her cheeks. "Have I been too demanding?"

"I've enjoyed every minute," he assured her.

She grinned back. "I can't remember when I've had this much fun."

"I'm glad." He glanced ruefully at the clock on the bedside table. "Our plane leaves in six hours. I suppose we should get some real sleep."

"I suppose," she returned with a mock pout. A playfulness spread over her face. "Of course we can sleep on the plane."

Amusement gleamed in his eyes. "True."

"First one into bed gets to be on top this time." She laughed out loud as they both rose and dove for the mattress.

Capturing her in his arms, Peter's expression suddenly became serious. "You could stay in my...our home in Oregon while I'm gone. It'd be safer for you there."

She recalled his mention of snakes and gigantic insects. But the thought of being parted from him pushed them from her mind. "No way. We made a deal and I plan to stick to it. Besides I want to see just exactly what you do to earn a living."

"I told you. I search for valuable mineral deposits."

She kissed his shoulder. "And what are you searching for this time?"

"Gold or gemstones," he replied, nuzzling her neck.

"Sounds interesting."

"Not as interesting as exploring you," he said gruffly and drew her to him.

Chapter Twelve

Two days later Ellen and Peter arrived at the hacienda of Señor Varjueze in the mountainous region of Guatemala. The next morning a helicopter transported them further into the mountains where several of Señor Varjueze's men were waiting, equipped with food and camping supplies, to accompany them on their search.

A tall, lanky man in his early forties, who looked to be a mixture of Mayan and Spanish descent, greeted them when they disembarked. "I am Carlos Gomez, Señor Varjueze's foreman," he introduced himself. "I and my men will see to your needs." His smile of greeting changed to a concerned frown as his gaze came to rest on Ellen. "This will be a difficult trek. The jungle can be very inhospitable. There are poisonous snakes. Spiders. Insects. And we will be cutting our own trails."

"My husband has explained all of that to me," she replied, recalling Peter's attempt to convince her to wait for him at the hacienda. "I'm sure I can handle it."

Carlos looked to Peter for help.

"She's made up her mind." A part of him admired her determination. Another was worried that she had not taken his description of what lay ahead seriously enough. "We can always arrange for the helicopter to come pick her up if she changes it."

Carlos said something in Spanish. Peter nodded. Ellen wasn't certain what had transpired between them, but from their expressions she guessed it had something to do with women being difficult or unreasonable. She didn't care. She spoke no Spanish. If she'd stayed at the hacienda, she would have been in a strange country, surrounded by strangers, most of whom she could not communicate with. "Shall we go?" she asked, picking up her backpack and pulling it on.

Carlos again cast Peter a worried look. Peter responded with an "I can't stop her" shrug and picked up his backpack. Ellen gave them both an "I don't care what you think" look and stood ready to proceed.

As Peter had warned, the jungle was hot, buggy and the going rough. A few hours later, her sweat-soaked clothing clinging to her, her arms tired from slapping at bugs and her legs beginning to ache from exercise they were not used to, she questioned her wisdom in coming. Glancing to her left, she saw a snake dangling from a branch of a tree. Her breath locked in her throat, and she froze in mid-stride.

"Are you beginning to regret coming along?" Peter asked, stopping behind her and following her line of vision.

She looked up at him and her fear subsided. "No," she said, and resumed walking. What amazed her was that this was true. In spite of the snake, the heat, the insects and the tiredness, she was glad to be there. It was all part of the adventure, she reasoned. Beside, lately she hadn't been behaving like her rational self so why should she start now?

It was mid-afternoon the next day when she was forced to face one truth about her behavior. She was sitting on a boulder waiting for Peter to come out of a small cave he'd squirmed into several minutes earlier.

She'd wanted to go in with him, but he'd put his foot down, insisting that he alone would enter. Caves were, he'd told her, unpredictable. It could be that it never got wider than the narrow opening he'd found. "Going into rat holes is why I get paid the big bucks," he'd said. "You will wait out here with Carlos and the others."

"You'll be careful?" she'd asked worriedly.

He'd grinned at her concern. "I'm always careful." Then he'd kissed her lightly and left.

Now as the minutes ticked by and he hadn't come back out, her nerves grew more and more tense and she was forced to admit that she hadn't refused to stay behind at the hacienda because she didn't want to be left alone among strangers. She'd refused to stay because she hadn't wanted to be parted from Peter. But was it love or lust?

Wrapping her arms around her legs, she rested her chin on her knees. Even as they'd exchanged their vows, she'd admitted to herself that she didn't expect this marriage to last. She'd married Peter because she'd wanted to be married and because she'd never felt such a strong attraction to a man before. But she had expected, as he'd predicted, that one morning she'd wake up and wonder what in the world she was doing in his bed. So far, however, that hadn't happened. So far, the sight of him continued to bring joy and excitement.

"But then, even lust takes time to fade," she muttered under her breath. And maybe this panic she was feeling was because she wouldn't want anyone to die in the blackness of that cave.

Her jaw tightened with resolve. If he wasn't out in another minute, she was going in after him! Her gaze shifted to her watch, and she observed the second hand move slowly around the dial. When it hit twelve, she slid off the boulder and started toward the entrance.

Halfway there, she came to an abrupt halt as a burlap collection bag was tossed out, followed by Peter's head and shoulders, then the rest of him. Her body felt weak with relief.

Scrambling to his feet, he strung the collection bag on his shoulder and began brushing off the dirt and dust he'd accumulated in the cave. "We'll continue north," he told Carlos. Carlos nodded and motioned for his men to begin hacking a trail.

Ellen took a deep breath to give herself time to regain control over her jangled nerves. Then, unable to remain silent, but not wanting him to guess how worried she'd been, she said dryly, "You certainly took your time."

"Miss me?" A playful lightness in his voice masked the fact that her answer meant more to him than he wanted to admit.

"Yes," she answered honestly.

Peter experienced a rush of pleasure and grinned. "I like the sound of that."

And she liked making him smile. "Did you find anything of interest."

He kissed her lightly. "Nothing more interesting than you." For the umpteenth time he cautioned himself not to begin to think this marriage would last. And when she wanted out he'd free her, but he knew he wouldn't be able to easily forget her.

A warm glow that had nothing to do with the jungle heat spread through Ellen. She grinned back, and in a thick Southern drawl said, "You do say the sweetest things."

Maybe she was learning to love him, Peter thought. He couldn't deny any longer that he'd fallen hard for her. In the past he'd always been able to block out everything but his work, but even in the dark depths of that cave, she'd been on his mind. *Don't get your hopes up,* his cautious voice warned. He'd been burned before. He motioned toward the path the men had cut. "We'd better get going before the others leave us behind."

Nodding, she preceded him into the jungle.

Several days later, propped on an elbow, Ellen stared down at Peter lying on his sleeping bag. He looked calm and confident, while she was fighting the threat of nausea brought on by fear. "*You're* going to be doing some blasting tomorrow?"

On their fourth day in the jungle, he'd called the helicopter to come pick them up. When it arrived, he'd had the pilot fly them along the path of a dry riverbed while he took aerial snapshots. Then he'd called a break, and everyone had returned by air to the hacienda for a couple of days. Now they were again in the jungle. For two days they'd followed the riverbed to reach a cliff face. She'd noticed that they'd brought back some explosives, but she'd never dreamed he was the one who would be using them. "Don't you have an expert you call in for that sort of thing?"

"I am the expert." He hadn't meant to frighten her, but he had to admit his hopes that she was learning to care for him were bolstered by the depth of her concern.

Normally his assurances served to ease Ellen's mind. This time they didn't. "You never said anything about blowing up things," she accused.

He gave her a wry look. "You didn't expect me to use a pickax all of the time, did you?"

"No, not just a pickax but not dynamite, either," she returned.

"I'm not using dynamite. I'm using plastique." Reaching up, he combed his fingers into her hair, cupping her head in his hand. "A person could get the impression that you're beginning to have some pretty deep feelings for me."

His touch made her want to purr with pleasure, but she wasn't yet prepared to admit how deeply she was beginning to care. She'd never believed real love could bloom so quickly. A part of her still suspected her feelings were born more from lust that an honest emotional commitment. "I only just found a husband. I'm not ready to be a widow."

He was expecting too much too soon, he told himself. "Tomorrow will be fun," he said, hiding his disappointment. "I think I've found the source I've been looking for."

"Source?" she asked, trying not to picture him lying injured in a pile of rocky rubble.

He pulled a long yellowish rock out of a collection bag lying near his side and held it up for her inspection.

"Most women's eyes light up when they see gold," he chided.

"Not even gold is worth risking your life for," she retorted, unable to stop the churning in her stomach.

The thought that his occupation could cause her to refuse to let her feelings for him grow, occurred to him. The concern she'd expressed that had so pleased him, now worried him. "It's what I do, Ellen. And I do it well. There is really no need for you to worry."

"Just be careful," she demanded curtly.

"I will," he promised, thinking that she was the most dangerous chance he'd ever taken. Somehow, he had to convince her that they belonged together forever.

Ellen stood with the rest of the men, a safe distance from the base of the cliff. Peter had rappelled from the top and was stopping at various distances to place the charges as he made his way to the base. When he'd refused to even allow any of the men to hike to the top of the cliff with him to help carry his equipment and supplies, she'd known then that there was a much greater danger involved than he'd wanted her to suspect. Peter, she'd learned during this trek, didn't mind facing danger himself, but he refused to put any of those in his care in harm's way.

"Do not worry," Carlos said encouragingly. "They say he is the best and the luckiest."

She hoped that whoever "they" were, were right. Visions of a premature explosion bringing the cliff down on top of Peter were causing her stomach to knot. She glanced at her watch. He'd been at it for nearly an hour. "How long does this kind of thing take?" she asked.

Carlos shrugged. "I am not an expert with explosives. It will take as long as it takes."

Feeling faint, Ellen realized she'd been holding her breath. She drew in a lungful of air while straining her eyes for any sign of trouble. Suddenly she noticed that Peter was completing his descent. As he reached the foot of the cliff, she breathed a sigh of relief.

After retrieving his climbing equipment, he started toward her, trailing wire along with him. Reaching her, he attached the wire to a small plunger box. "You do the honors," he said, hoping that making her a part of his discovery would reduce her fears.

She read the excited anticipation in his eyes and, now that he was standing safely beside her, she had to admit to a beginning tingle of excitement herself. Accepting control of the plunger, she pushed it down. A rumble sounded, then the cliff face crumbled and came down. Glints of gold sparkled in the sunlight.

Ellen grinned. "Let's go see what you uncovered."

Peter held her back. As much as he wanted her to join in his excitement, he would not risk her safety. "I'll go alone."

"Why can't I go with you?" she asked, already knowing the answer but not wanting to hear it.

"There could still be loose rock." He kissed her lightly. "I'm just going to take a quick look."

"A quick look," she stipulated as he walked away from her.

Again her stomach knotted as she waited. Although it was only a few minutes, his "quick look" felt like forever. When he returned, the triumph of a job well done glistened in his eyes. "You can contact Señor Varjueze and tell him to contact his mining experts," he informed Carlos. "It's my guess we've found the mother lode."

Carlos grinned. "I'll contact him immediately."

Ellen didn't think a hot bath had ever felt so good. Señor Varjueze had sent a helicopter to pick up her and Peter as soon as Carlos had contacted him with the good news. Now they were at his hacienda.

She'd gone directly to their rooms to bathe while Peter met with Varjueze. The urge to linger in the water all afternoon was strong, but she knew Peter would want to bathe, too. She was toweling dry when he knocked on the door, then entered.

"You smell good," he said, sniffing her neck.

Curls of pleasure wove through her. "And you smell ripe."

"Will you stay and wash my back?" he coaxed.

"Is a wife's work never done?" she teased, glad of any excuse to be near him. Fastening the towel around herself, she started a fresh tub of bathwater while he began to undress.

As she soaped his hair, the fear that she could have lost him today caused her to tremble. Trying not to think about it, she playfully pushed him under the water to rinse the soap out. In return, as he emerged, he gave his hair a fling spraying her with water.

"As wet as I'm getting, I might as well be in there with you," she quipped, starting to work on his back.

"An excellent idea," he growled and in the next instant she found herself being pulled in on top of him.

Later as she lay beside him on their bed, she told herself to keep her own counsel, but the events of the day weighed too heavily upon her. Turning onto her side, she levered herself on an elbow so that she could see his face. "I learned something about myself today," she said.

The serious, anxious expression on her face caused the worry that was always at the back of his mind to surface. His jaw firmed. He'd never been one to turn away from the truth, no matter how much he didn't want to hear it. "Is this where you tell me that you suddenly woke up and wondered what the hell you were doing in the middle of nowhere, with a stranger you barely know, leading a life that's been exciting but not the kind you want to pursue for the rest of your days?"

"You're not a stranger to me anymore." Her expression remaining solemn. "I know you to be a decent, honest, good man."

The words *decent, honest,* and *good* echoed in Peter's mind as he braced himself for a "Dear John" speech. He'd known this marriage probably wouldn't last, he reminded himself. But the thought of losing her shook him to the core. His jaw tensed with purpose. He wasn't going to give her up easily. He'd find a way to convince her to give him more time to prove he could be the husband she wanted.

"I've never been so terrified of anything as I was when you were setting those explosives," Ellen continued levelly.

"I told you I knew what I was doing."

"Yes, you did. And Carlos told me that you were not only the best but the luckiest. That still didn't keep me from almost throwing up from sheer terror."

"You'll get used to it," he said, his arm wrapping around her, drawing her closer to him.

She grimaced ruefully. "I'm going to have to."

He saw the brown of her eyes soften.

"What I realized today is that you're definitely not a rebound or wild oats. I'm in love with you," she finished, nervously searching his face for his reaction to this declaration. "Do you think there's a chance you could learn to feel the same about me?"

His jaw relaxed and his gaze warmed. "I do. I told myself I was only marrying you to save you from yourself—" a crooked grin suddenly played at one corner of his mouth "—and to satisfy the physical attraction I felt for you. But on the day of our wedding, when the minister asked us if we wanted to go through with the union, the fear that you would say you'd been having second thoughts and wanted out had my stomach in knots. That was when I realized how much I honestly wanted you to be a part of my life...that I was hopelessly in love with you."

Ellen grinned with relief. "I do like the sound of that. As much as you scared me today, I do love exploring with you."

He laughed at the double entendre in her voice.

A couple of days later, Ellen stared out of the windshield of Peter's truck at his "cabin" in the mountains. She'd begun to suspect her husband had not been entirely honest with her when a chartered jet had been waiting for them in Los Angeles to fly them to Oregon.

"When the man at the gas station referred to this as 'your' mountain, he meant that literally, didn't he?" she asked, her gaze moving from the massive log house in front of her to the forest beyond.

"I own most of it," Peter replied, smiling at her stunned expression.

Confusion showed on her face. "You said your first wife left you for a man with money."

"I said my first wife was only interested in money," he corrected. "Mine, to be exact."

"Oh," she returned weakly.

"When I was twenty-one I bought some property in Alaska, gambling that it had potential for being rich in natural resources. I struck gold. Next I invested in some land in Mexico and found an emerald mine on the property. That's when I knew I had a knack for finding that sort of thing. The press learned of my success and started calling me the man with the Midas touch. That's how Nancy found me. After my experience with her, I decided that I might have a Midas touch for finding precious metals and gems but I sure didn't have one for finding a wife."

He kissed her. "I was wrong. You've turned out to be worth your weight in gold."

A sudden thought crossed her mind. "You were the anonymous Good Samaritan who bought the new plane for the Pyresses."

"They needed a little helping hand."

"And then you saved me from Charles."

He grinned with playful lechery. "They say a good deed should never go unrewarded. And I'm in the mood to be rewarded."

"I wouldn't want to prove whoever 'they' are wrong." The joy of knowing she was exactly where she belonged swept through her as she left the truck and walked with him to the porch.

After unlocking the door, he scooped her up in his arms. "Welcome home, Mrs. Whitley."

She laughed lightly. "My mother will be relieved to know we have hot and cold running water and electricity," she said as he carried her over the threshold.

* * * * * *

This April
DEBBIE MACOMBER

takes readers to the Big Sky and beyond...

MONTANA

At her grandfather's request, Molly packs up her kids and returns to his ranch in Sweetgrass, Montana.

But when she arrives, she finds a stranger, Sam Dakota, working there. Molly has questions: What exactly is he doing there? Why doesn't the sheriff trust him? Just *who* is Sam Dakota? These questions become all the more critical when her grandfather tries to push them into marriage....

Moving to the state of Montana is one thing; entering the state of matrimony is quite another!

Available in April 1998 wherever books are sold.

MIRA

MDM434